"I'm afraid there's nothing we can do, Nick."

There was only one way Nick could prevent his family from losing Fern. "We can marry."

Fern's eyes widened. *"Nay,* you don't mean that." She shook her head.

"I do, Fern. I don't want you to go. And Bethany and Josh—can we break their hearts?"

She was still shaking her head, as if she hadn't heard him right. But she hadn't actually said no, had she?

"Think, Fern. This way you can keep your vow to Charity. That's what you want, isn't it?"

"What I want?" The puzzled look on her face suggested she hadn't much considered what she wanted.

He knew the one thing she *didn't* want—him as anything more than a friend.

"You belong with the *kinner.* And they with you. This is the best I can do for all of us. The closest way to keep our vows to Charity."

That was the reason behind this desperation pounding through his blood, wasn't it? To honor his promise. To treat Fern with the respect she deserved...

Amy Grochowski's deep appreciation for the Amish faith and way of life stems from six years of living and working with a Beachy Amish family, as well as her own Anabaptist roots. After a nursing career of over twenty years, Amy is now fulfilling her long-awaited dream career as an author of inspirational romance. She is also a full-time homeschool mom for her two sons, one of whom has autism spectrum disorder. She lives with her family in the bustling foothills of North Carolina. Learn more at amygrochowski.com.

Books by Amy Grochowski

Love Inspired

The Amish Nanny's Promise

Visit the Author Profile page at LoveInspired.com.

The Amish Nanny's Promise

Amy Grochowski

LOVE INSPIRED
INSPIRATIONAL ROMANCE

LOVE INSPIRED®
INSPIRATIONAL ROMANCE

Recycling programs
for this product may
not exist in your area.

ISBN-13: 978-1-335-59823-3

The Amish Nanny's Promise

Copyright © 2023 by Amy Grochowski

For questions and comments about the quality of this book, please contact us at CustomerService@Harlequin.com.

Love Inspired
22 Adelaide St. West, 41st Floor
Toronto, Ontario M5H 4E3, Canada
www.LoveInspired.com

Printed in U.S.A.

And above all these things put on charity,
which is the bond of perfectness.
—*Colossians* 3:14

For my beloved husband, David,
who believed in me, married me and every day
since has supported me to become the woman
God created me to be. I wish everyone in the
world had a life partner like you.

Chapter One

Too soon, Nick Weaver opened his eyes to the shadowy light of predawn. Once again, he'd lain awake for hours, only to succumb to sleep shortly before his day was to begin. He pushed aside the handmade quilt, swung his legs over the side of the bed and sat up.

He raked his fingers through his beard and then his thick, dark hair. Somehow, he had to be awake and somewhat presentable before Fern Beiler came to the house. Over the past two years, his late wife's cousin had arrived like clockwork every morning of the week, except for the Sabbath, to care for his *kinner* while he ran his Amish grocery store.

And he supposed it was that routine that kept him going—second, of course, to his love for eight-year-old *dochter*, Bethany, and three-year-old *sohn*, Josh.

When he'd promised Charity to keep her memory alive for the *kinner*, he'd not imagined how difficult a vow it would be to abide by. The children had been so young and already their memories of their *mamm* were all but gone.

He'd promised because it seemed like the right thing to do, for one.

But he also knew Charity's worst fears were for her children. And no wonder, the way her *dat* had replaced her *mamm*, when he remarried and moved away from their small Virginia mountain town to another Amish church district in the Shenandoah Valley. Charity had been left here in the highlands of Promise, Virginia, and lived with her grandmother Ada Beiler from infancy.

And so, Nick remained committed to staying single—at least until the *kinner* were older. And unlike most Amish, who rarely spoke of the deceased, he made certain to tell stories about their *mamm*, reminding them what she was like.

At first, that felt like enough. But on these long, sleepless nights, he feared he wasn't getting this right. Something was off-kilter— something Charity would've pinpointed, just like Nick knew when his inventory at the store needed adjusting or whether a new grocery item or Amish novelty would sell. But Charity wasn't here to guide where his instinct lacked.

He muffled a groan. Nothing would get solved by staying in bed. He rubbed at his eyes with the heel of his two palms before combing his fingers through the wavy tangle of his dark hair, then with a push against the mattress, he stood to meet the day.

The outline of his simple Amish bedroom came into focus around him. An arm's length away stood the chair where he'd left his pants and suspenders to dress quickly. His light blue shirt, though it looked dark in the dim light, hung on a peg on the wall behind the chair.

Nick tiptoed in socked feet down the hallway. Stopping at the door to his eight-year-old daughter's room, he peeked inside. Bethany's long black hair lay in waves across her pillow. She slept on her back with her hands tucked under her head. Nick's mini-me, Charity had called her.

Beside her a toddler-sized lump moved under the covers. Nick smiled. Josh began every night in his own room and somehow ended up with his sister by morning. He bore a strong resemblance to his mother's kinfolk.

The blond curls of his baby days were turning darker, to match his chocolate brown eyes.

With care not to wake them, Nick headed to the washroom. Leaning over the sink, he cupped his hands under the flowing spigot. The splash of ice-cold water against his face shocked the sleepless night from his system.

Downstairs in the kitchen, he fumbled around for the percolator. The cranky pot always gave him a fit. After a few weeks of drinking gritty *kaffi*, Fern had taken over and began preparing the pot before she went home each day. Since then, all he'd had to do was heat the stove and the *kaffi* practically made itself.

He pulled two mugs out of the cupboard and the cream from the icebox. From the window above the kitchen sink, he watched the horizon burst into a deep red along the crest of Promise Mountain. Soon the sun would follow above the ridgetop.

Red sky at morning, sailors take warning. So went the saying about bad weather to come after such a crimson sunrise, but the forecast in yesterday's paper had called for clear skies all week.

He strummed his fingers on the counter. It was still too dark to see all the way to the house across the road to Ada Beiler's cottage, where Fern had lived with her grandmother since he and Charity married.

A prick of worry niggled at his thoughts.

It bothered him that Fern traveled alone from her nursing duty at the Schrocks' to her grandmother's house at night. Promise had a reputation for being a safe community. But nighttime brought out the occasional trouble-maker, even to their cozy Blue Ridge moun-tain hamlet. When he'd mentioned as much to Ada, he earned a sharp rebuke.

"Those home-care jobs are how she supports herself. Fern is not your *frau*." As if he didn't know. As if he wasn't constantly reminded that everyone else thought she ought to be. *Nay*, Fern was certainly not his wife. But she and Charity had been as close as sisters. Charity would be sorely disappointed if Nick didn't at least try to look out for her cousin. The bottom line was that Fern ought to be safe. He didn't have to be her husband to make sure she was escorted home safely.

It wouldn't be the first time he'd stepped in. Ada certainly hadn't minded fifteen years ago when Nick had been looking out for her granddaughter. If *Gott* hadn't changed Nick's course that afternoon… Nick shuddered at the memory. He couldn't bear the thought of how much damage the fire might have done to Fern that day if he hadn't found her when he did.

Charity had a way of making him feel like a hero after that, which, of course, he wasn't. He'd merely used the common sense the Lord gave him.

Fern, on the other hand, had withdrawn from him—from everyone. She'd only come out of her shell years later by caring for the sick in their community. Maybe because she knew better than most how they were suffering.

A sizzle sounded from the stove where the percolator boiled. He wasn't used to drinking his morning *kaffi* alone on a weekday. And he didn't much like it.

Bang. The familiar slam of the back door set everything back to right.

"I sure am glad to smell that *kaffi*." Fern's familiar voice drifted in from the mudroom. "Did you oversleep?"

Hardly.

Grabbing a pot holder, Nick removed the steaming carafe from the heat and poured their drinks. Then, just as Fern came through the mudroom into the kitchen, he added the healthy dollop of cream he knew she liked.

"Gut mariye." He pushed her mug toward

the chair where she usually sat, then leaned against the back of his chair, thankful the dim light hid how relieved he was to see her.

"Are you going to stay in the dark, Nick?" She lit the kerosene lamp above the table and plopped down in the chair. Her hands wrapped around the mug before she blew out a slow, tired breath. "I think I need the entire pot this morning."

"I didn't sleep so well last night, either," Nick confessed.

Her mouth opened, as if she was going to reply, but she shook her head instead.

Nick watched a strand of her nut-brown hair fall across her face as she bent her head toward the steaming liquid. Her long and slender fingers encompassed the mug gracefully. She took a sip, then closed her eyes for a moment and sighed.

"No frost this morning, but it's still cold out there, I reckon." He drank the first mouth-melting swallow of his own.

"Not so bad as it has been. I noticed the daffodils poking through the ground yesterday. Definitely nippy, though." She rubbed the tip of her nose. Again, he thought she was about to say something more, but she returned her focus to her mug.

She looked so different from Charity, even though they were first cousins. Fern's eyes were as dark as the *kaffi* before he'd added the cream. He couldn't tell where her pupils ended and the eye color began. Where Charity had been fair, rosy and lightly freckled, Fern's complexion was smooth and ivory—until summer when the sun darkened her skin several shades and her hair lightened to the amber of pure maple syrup. The scar from the accident that she kept mostly hidden had faded. In fact, if he didn't know it was there behind her ear and along her neck, he'd probably never notice it now.

"What?" she asked, returning his stare. "*Ach*, I guess you're wondering why I was late."

Not at that exact moment, *nay*.

"No matter. It's not like you're an employee." Another area of failure on his part that made him as uncomfortable as her walking home alone at night. He was keenly aware some folks believed he was taking advantage of Fern's natural tendency to serve others. As if he hadn't offered—more times than he could count—to pay Fern for her time caring for the children. She always stubbornly refused.

"Ada had a few words to say before I left this morning." She swiped at the hair falling from her prayer *kapp*.

"A few?" Nick had never known Ada to have less than a mouthful to spill.

Fern's gaze caught his. A grin trembled at the corner of her lips.

Nick downed the rest of his drink to hide his pleasure at almost making her laugh.

What was he doing? Something that felt dangerously close to flirting. And with Fern. He pushed his chair back and stood.

"I best get to the store." As he avoided the confused look on Fern's face, his eyes landed on the surprise he'd saved for Bethany this morning. Now he'd messed that up, too, and would miss the pleasure on his daughter's face. "I brought home an extra hand-pie yesterday for Bethany's lunch. Can you put it in her pail for school today?" He waited long enough for her nod of agreement, then strode to the sink, rinsed his cup and headed out the way Fern had just come.

"Nick?" she called after him with an understandable question in her voice. "Aren't you going to eat breakfast?"

Another task Fern performed because he'd botched up his efforts at that, too. "*Nay*, I'll eat one of those granola bars down at the store."

He hadn't even turned around to address

her. His conscience reprimanded him for being rude. Fern had done nothing wrong.

Looking over his shoulder, he attempted to add some cheer to his tone. "I have an extra-busy morning. Besides, I didn't dare attempt making myself eggs and burn the house down."

Fern's hand flew to her neck and the spot where her prayer *kapp* covered her ear and the horrible scar from the accident. But it was the pitiful little cry she made that tore his heart.

"I didn't mean… Fern, that's not what I was thinking." Could he mess this day up any more?

"I know." She waved him off, but he still saw the sting of his words in the drooping of her eyelashes. "I'm just…a little extra sensitive this morning, is all."

He took a step closer to her, then paused.

"*Denki*, Fern, for being so forgiving. It was a *dummkopf* thing to say." He waited for her nod, then headed straight for the door.

He was truly sorry, but he needed to leave before he said or did anything to make matters worse. He also had to get more sleep.

Fern couldn't let Nick leave, not now that she'd finally gotten up the courage to talk to him. And today, of all mornings, he was running off almost as soon as she arrived.

For months, she and Nick had ignored the nagging of their families and the church elders about marriage—or their lack in that department. At least, she and Nick sure hadn't talked about it.

The hints began about a year after Charity's passing. And now, another year later, nothing had changed between her and Nick and the whispered hints were turning to full-on meddlesome threats.

She had to talk to Nick before the bishop and her *grossmammi* got to him first.

"Wait." She called after him as she ran across the kitchen. The mudroom was empty. He'd already left. She yanked the back door open and stepped out again into the cool morning. "Nick!"

He was already halfway through the yard with his long, sure strides. Fern ran a few feet after him and called again. This time he stopped and turned to face her.

"Please, stay a little longer. I need to talk to you." He didn't look angry, even though he'd marched off in a hurry. She wasn't sure what was going on with him this morning. If anything, he seemed confused. And what she had to say wasn't going to help. "Can't you come eat breakfast?"

She shivered.

This would go much better inside. And thankfully he agreed, following her back to the house.

"I could use a second cup of *kaffi*. How about you?" he said as he held the door open.

"*Ya*," she answered just as a sleepy-eyed Bethany wandered through from the kitchen. Like every morning, she did her chores before breakfast and dressing for school.

"*Gut mariye*," Bethany said as she wrapped her curly dark hair into a band to hold it back. While her brother resembled their fair-headed *mamm*, Bethany took after Nick with her dark locks that fought to be free of any pins or *kapps* all the way to her long legs that threatened to outgrow Fern too soon. She was not only tall for her age but exceptionally athletic—something neither Fern nor Charity had ever been, but her mother would certainly have admired.

Bethany glanced over at her *dat*, then back to Fern. "I was going to get the eggs. Did I oversleep?"

"*Nay*." Fern pulled the girl into a hug and kissed the top of her head. She was at a loss to explain why she and Nick had been outside.

And clearly, they hadn't done the chores as they had neither eggs nor milk in hand.

Nick squeezed past them without an explanation, either.

Fern reached for the egg basket still sitting by the door and handed it to Bethany. "There's enough left for breakfast. You can milk Susie and then bring in the eggs. No need for an extra trip."

"All right." Bethany shrugged into her coat without any questions and headed toward the chicken coop.

If Fern was going to talk to Nick, she'd better get on with it. Bethany's chores wouldn't take very long, and little Josh would come running as soon as the smell of bacon wafted up to his room.

Nick was waiting at the counter by the stove. He handed her another cup of *kaffi*. "What is it that you need to tell me? Is it the *kinner*?"

Of course his first concern would jump to his children. It was a fear they held in common, ever since Charity's sudden illness and passing. And her main worry this morning was all about the *kinner*, but not as he feared. Nothing was wrong with Bethany and Josh.

Not yet.

"*Nay*, Josh and Bethany are doing fine."

He blew out a deep breath.

She passed Nick a frying pan to set on the stove beside him, then she began cracking eggs into a bowl. Nick watched her. She had to get to the point.

"The bishop is coming to see Ada this afternoon. She didn't give me a reason, but she's been acting very strange the past couple of weeks, since…" This was the part she dreaded to mention—the part about Charity's father, the man who had married her grandmother's only *dochter*. After she died tragically in a buggy accident, he left their infant *boppli* with *Grossmammi* to raise, and he'd rarely been heard from since. "She received a letter from Thomas Miller and has been very secretive about what he had to say."

"I reckon the man ought to communicate with Ada. He was once her son-in-law, even if that was many years ago." Nick's mouth set in a straight line. Likely he was attempting to do what she had—convince himself it didn't mean anything. Only a feeling that something serious was happening kept nagging at her. "So, what do you think that has to do with the bishop coming to visit your *grossmammi*?"

"I don't know exactly. But, Rhoda came by yesterday." Fern watched Nick's brow rise at the mention of his *mamm*. "She asked a lot of questions about things she thought she ought to know so she can help out here sometimes."

Nick looked more confused than ever. "What kind of questions? *Mamm* knows how to care for a house and her own *grosskinner*."

Exactly. "I think it was more of a warning. A kind one. As if I was supposed to understand something. And there's only one thing I know of."

Please don't make me spell it out for you. The humiliation of her family and the bishop joining forces to push her into marriage was bad enough without having to explain it outright.

Fern whipped the eggs, waiting for Nick to reach his own conclusions. She traded spots with him, so she could lay the bacon in the now-hot skillet.

Nick turned to face her and leaned against the counter. A storm seemed to be waging in the gray blue of his eyes.

Fern tugged at the corner of her prayer *kapp* and focused on her task at the stove. Whatever Nick was thinking, he was keeping it to himself. But he must have some idea of what was going on.

Poor Fern. She'll never marry unless we make it happen.

Maybe those weren't the exact words of their families in recent months, but the sentiment was the same as always when the elders and her family stepped in to *help* her. But why now? She was fine. In fact, she'd been doing perfectly well on her own for a long time now.

She'd never been happier than when she was caring for Bethany and Josh while Nick ran his Amish grocery during the day. Why couldn't her *grossmammi* and the bishop see she was doing what she wanted to be doing? No one needed to pity her—or force marriage on her. Or Nick.

Beneath her fingertips the rough line of skin that ran from her ear to her shoulder was the ever-present reminder of their reasons. Ever since the accident that left her scarred at age fourteen, they'd all been extra protective. Even now, fifteen years later, they were trying to fix her life for her.

Poor Fern.

Even though she'd proved herself capable of handling responsibility after years of caring for the community's sick and elderly, the old whispers after the fire still haunted her. *Didn't she know better? No man will ever trust her to keep his house. What a shame...*

But Charity had trusted her.

Caring for her *kinner* was the closest Fern was likely to ever come to having a family of her own. Not only were the children her last connection to their mother, she'd promised Charity she would care for them. Fern hadn't fully understood her cousin's insistence, but never once had she regretted giving Charity her word to watch closely over Bethany and Josh and bring them up with the love she wanted them to have.

And Fern meant to keep her promise.

"Fern?" The sound of Nick's voice startled her from her thoughts. "I've no intention of changing anything here. Is that what you're afraid of?"

"*Ya*. That's the gist of it, I think." If they tried to convince Nick the right thing to do in their situation was to marry Fern, she knew he wouldn't.

Not once in all their lives had Nick ever thought of her in *that way*. *Nay*, she was sure he hadn't. If they pushed Nick to the wall about their arrangement, he'd find someone else to watch his children before he'd marry her. Even his *mamm* must believe he'd refuse. Why else would she have said what she did? "Rhoda could care for the *kinner*, I know. And maybe it is selfish, but I love them, Nick."

His throat bobbed with a deep swallow and his gaze fixed on the other side of the room. "Well, then, as long as you're willing and happy to help with Bethany and Josh, there's no reason to fix what ain't broke."

"I'm not sure they see it that way." She was glad they agreed that things should stay as they were, but he made it sound so easy.

Making her promise to her cousin had been easy. Not only did she love Charity and her *kinner*, but helping Nick after her death was the least Fern could do for the man who'd once saved her from a far worse end to that fire than a scar. A memory they'd both been reminded of that very morning.

The bacon sputtered in the pan. She grabbed a fork to turn the pieces over when warm little arms wrapped around her leg.

"Hay-woe, Fuh-nee." Josh's freckled face was turned up toward her. With a free hand, she rubbed the top of his strawberry blond head.

Her heart squeezed tight in the center of her chest.

"Try not to worry, Fern." Nick squatted in front of her and scooped Josh into his arms. "I'll speak with Ada and the bishop about this. We'll work it out somehow."

Fern pressed a hand against her midsection as an ominous sense that her life was about to change churned inside her.

With both families and the bishop determined not to let their current arrangement continue, what did Nick think he could say or do?

She prayed Nick was right. Surely, they could find a solution to this expectation of their families and the church. They'd work it out, somehow. They had to.

For Charity. For the children.

Chapter Two

❧

Nick smiled at an *Englisch* customer approaching the checkout counter at his grocery store.

"Here, let me help you with that." Nick reached for the heavy load of goods balanced precariously in the middle-aged woman's arms.

"Thank you." She released a five-pound sack of oatmeal into one of his waiting hands. "I should've gotten a basket, but I only intended to get some of your amazing homemade sausage."

Nick nodded. At least a dozen times or more a day, he'd heard similar stories.

After he completed the sale and bagged her groceries, the woman offered a promise to return soon. The fancy grocery stores down in the Shenandoah Valley paid for expensive advertising and marketing to sell goods the way products flew off the shelves at Weaver's Amish Store.

Ya, tonight, he'd remember to thank *Gott* for His continued blessing on a humble Amish store owner and his simple mountain-town business in rural Promise, Virginia. And maybe he'd sleep better than last night. Then again, maybe not, depending on whatever business was brewing with the bishop. The sooner he dealt with that the better, apparently.

The bell above the store entrance jingled.

"Hello, *Dat*," Bethany and Josh called out in unison. In a flash, they were both behind the counter. "*Denki* for the fried pie in my lunch today," said Bethany.

"You're welcome." Nick bent down to give them each a hug and reached for the candy jar he kept just for them. Josh's eyes grew wide. Usually he was bouncing on his toes in anticipation. But today, he appeared tired.

Fern had mentioned that getting Josh to sleep in the afternoon was becoming more difficult. Nick looked up to ask whether Josh had napped today, only she wasn't there.

"Where's Fern?" he asked.

"On da porch…" Josh said as he plunged his

hand into the candy jar. "She said she was too old to run so far."

"She ran all the way here?" Nick asked.

"She said something about it being the bishop's fault." Bethany took her turn choosing a sweet. "And something about *Grossmammi*, too, but I couldn't understand her. She said it didn't matter and to come inside without her."

"I see. I'll be right back." Nick walked around the counter to the door. "Your cousin Cassie is in the back. If you stay out from underfoot, you may go watch her ice the cakes."

They scampered off toward the bakery section, and Nick went outside to find Fern.

He found her on the farthest corner of the porch that stretched the length of the building. Her back was to him and her arms stretched wide with her hands pressed against the railing.

His years of marriage had taught him to recognize when a woman was upset. This wasn't Fern flustered, like he'd imagined from Josh's explanation. Something was wrong. Really wrong.

"Fern?" He edged a little closer but didn't want to invade her space without permission. "Can I do something?"

Her only answer was a shrug, so he dared a few steps closer.

She sighed and her shoulders sagged. "I promised."

He was directly beside her now. And she didn't appear to be out of breath, although her face was blotchy. He'd never seen Fern cry, but when she turned to face him directly, his guess was she'd been crying before he got out here.

"I promised her, Nick. And now I don't know how to keep it."

He had no idea what she was talking about, but he sure knew what she felt. "I have that struggle myself. Want to talk about it?"

She closed her eyes, the way she'd done that morning. He'd thought she was just enjoying the warmth of the *kaffi*. But this time, he was sure she was praying in that brief moment. "I think we don't have any choice but to talk about it, Nick. I was going to tell you this morning. Warn you, more like. But now... Now it's all out of control."

She was scaring him now. He'd never known her to fall apart like this. Fern held everything together after Charity passed. What could be worse than that? "What's out of control?"

"*Grossmammi* has the bishop convinced that—"

"Oh, Fern. Is that what this is about? I run the local grocery. I hear all the gossip that passes through this community. I do my best not to listen, but that's not possible all the time." It surprised him this was the first she'd heard of the whispers about how inappropriate their arrangement was. She obviously did a better job of ignoring gossip than he did. "Why don't you just let me pay you for caring for the *kinner*?"

A baffled expression crossed her face. "What would that solve?"

"Well, you'd just be like a nanny or a mother's helper. No one has a problem with those arrangements, do they?"

"A mother's helper is an unmarried Amish girl, *ya*, but she works for the mother, not the unmarried father, Nick. And it wouldn't make any difference to *Grossmammi*. She's taking me with her when she moves. And now Bishop Naaman agrees. Unless…" She sighed heavily. "He's over at Eli's right now. And then they are coming here to talk to you."

The part about the bishop and Eli, his brother who was also a minister, wasn't too shocking. He'd supposed he'd get a talking-to, eventually. And he'd figured he could handle it. After all, he and Fern weren't doing anything immoral.

But Ada was moving? And she was taking Fern with her? Now, that did throw him off his game. "What are you talking about? Taking you where?"

"*Grossmammi* says she's going to live with Uncle Titus down in central Virginia. She says the winters here are too hard on her now."

"Sounds reasonable." But he figured there was a catch. There always was with Ada. "But?"

"But…" Fern's stance relaxed a bit, as if he was slowly but finally catching on. "I can't stay at her cottage."

"Did she say why?" Nick had a sinking feeling this was related to the letter Fern mentioned earlier that morning. He'd been chewing on that bit of information about his absentee father-in-law all day, wondering what it had to do with anything.

Fern wiped at her eyes. "*Nay.* She was amazingly tight-lipped on that point."

This was strange, even for Ada. But he didn't think things really had to change so much. Some of the tension building up in his shoulders released. "Why leave with her? You could live with your parents, couldn't you?" Sure, she'd be a little farther away from the farmhouse than just across the lane at Ada's cottage, but not too far. Fern's *mamm* and *dat* lived right next door to his own parents. They'd grown up as neighbors. "It's a little farther for you to come to the house to care for the *kinner*, but we'll work it out."

"*Ya*, I would do so, but they want me to go with *Grossmammi*." She blew out a sigh, looking tired of explaining herself. "*Mamm* and *Dat* want me to take care of her. Uncle Titus has six children of his own, so his hands are full. And with *Grossmammi*, too..."

And they all thought Nick was taking advantage of Fern's good nature. His pulse speeded up at the thought. Surely, Fern wasn't really going to leave Promise altogether. "And the bishop agrees that you should go?"

"They won't be satisfied to let me stay, unless..." She couldn't seem to get the rest of her sentence out.

Poor Fern.

"*Ya*, I see where this is all going." Nick may have been a little dense up to this point, but he wasn't about to force her to repeat the phrase that humiliated her so much.

For the first time, he shared in her fear. And not because his *kaffi* would be gritty. *Nay*, Bethany and Josh would be devastated. He'd do anything to protect his *kinner* from more heartbreak. But he couldn't solve this—not in that way.

"Fern, I'm sorry. I can't.. I—"

"I'm not asking it of you!" Her widened brown eyes turned misty. "It's just that I promised."

"What promise, Fern?"

"To Charity. I promised her I'd take care of the *kinner*."

He rubbed at a knot tightening at the back of his neck. "And make sure they remembered her?"

Her brown eyes widened. "You knew?"

"*Nay*, I promised her, too."

She slumped against the railing. "What are we going to do?"

He should've known the day was coming when he'd have to explain this to Fern. But—until now—they'd shared an unspoken understanding that worked fine.

"Even if I…if we… Fern, I can't keep my promise to Charity and remarry now. That's all there is to it." Maybe not all. He'd expected if he remarried for it to be on his own terms, not Ada Beiler's. And he'd expected to choose the woman himself.

She nodded with a little sniff. He offered

her the handkerchief from his pocket, but she simply stared down at it.

"I hoped if I got to you first, that we might figure a way around this. There must be some way for both of us to keep our promises."

His *mamm* and others could help out with household duties, but the *kinner* were attached to Fern. A person you love couldn't just be replaced. He knew that all too well.

They'd both made promises to Charity for the children's sakes, but they couldn't continue to ignore their families and now the bishop, too. They'd put off the inevitable for too long.

"When the bishop and my brother come to see me, I will have to hear them out. If they insist that marriage is the only solution, I don't see what can be done. I cannot give them the outcome Ada desires. I am sorry. Truly, Fern, I do not want you to go."

"I never expected anything different from you, Nick. You know that, right? I love Josh and Bethany as much as I loved their *mamm*. If they were my own, I can't imagine how I could love them more. I know *Grossmammi* has her reasons, but I never dreamed the bishop would do this."

"And Eli." He was shocked, too. His brother was a fair-minded minister. And the bishop had been a rock-solid support when Charity passed. Nick never supposed he'd have a reason to doubt the man, much less oppose him. But this hard-line decision seemed out of character. "And Ada, she is this determined to take you with her?"

"She is. Is there nothing we can do—for the sake of the *kinner*?" The well of her unshed tears deepened. Nick knew how much Fern loved Bethany and Josh. Her love for them made him want to do anything he could for her. And saying goodbye to Fern would break their hearts. It was a cruel thing to do. He couldn't help that their *mamm* was taken from them. But this... Did he have a choice in this matter?

He couldn't see how.

"I wish there were another way."

"As do I." The sadness in her voice tore at his heart. "Will you send Bethany and Josh out to me? I don't think I could face anyone inside the store today."

"Of course." What a small thing, when she needed so much more from him. He jammed his hands into his pockets. "You believe Eli and Bishop Naaman will come today?"

She nodded.

"Well, they won't come until after closing,

or they may wait until tonight, after the *kinner* are in bed." He was thinking out loud and Fern had looked away, lost in her own thoughts.

He touched her elbow to draw her attention back. She turned halfway but didn't raise her eyes to his. He'd never known exactly how to comfort Fern. He'd botched it after he'd smothered the kitchen fire so long ago, too.

Gott, help me do a better job this time.

He stepped closer. Her downward gaze remained on his shoes rather than his face, but he plunged ahead.

"You shouldn't have to work tonight—not on top of all of this. I can have Cassie go see Esther Schrock and explain that you may not be able to come help tonight." That didn't seem like enough. Fern shouldn't have to go at all, not in her current state of turmoil. "I could even ask Cassie to consider helping Esther tonight to give you a rest." It wouldn't be a problem, Nick was certain. His brother, Eli, would understand why Nick asked his daughter to help.

She looked up at him, finally, with eyes that knew him through and through. "*Denki*, Nick. You always think of everything."

If that were true, they wouldn't be in this mess, but he didn't argue. They were both well aware he'd failed to think up a solution to the problem this time.

From their childhood days, church and family celebrations—and tragedies—all the way to this day, they'd always been neighbors and friends. He wasn't prepared for life without Fern Beiler in it.

What, he wondered helplessly, did *Gott* mean for him to do?

On his way to get the *kinner*, he grabbed a chicken potpie from the freezer section and gave it to Bethany to take to Fern. At least he could make supper a little easier for her tonight.

It wasn't near enough, though. He sent the children on their way, wishing he could live up to Fern's belief in him this once when it mattered so much to her—to the *kinner*.

To him.

Fern held Josh's hand on one side and Bethany's on the other as they crossed the intersection with the lane leading home. They'd all been quieter than usual. Funny how even a child could sense when something was wrong.

"How about a song?" She squeezed their hands before letting go after they were safely across the street.

"Jesus Wuvs Me." Josh announced the title of his favorite, and in a moment, all three of them were singing.

The children's innocent voices pealed the melody loud and sweet, restoring some strength to Fern's wounded spirit. By the final strain, they were climbing the front steps of Nick's old wooden-frame farmhouse.

Bethany handed Fern the frozen potpie she'd carried all the way down the main street through Promise. "*Dat* said you and *Gross-mammi* can eat with us tonight. Will you?"

"*Ya*, if she wants. Why don't you run and check with her? And don't forget to look both ways before crossing the lane." Rarely did anything other than a buggy travel down their lane off the main road, but good habits prevented accidents. A lesson Fern learned the hard way.

"*Ya*, I will." Bethany skipped away.

It wouldn't be the first time Ada and Fern joined Nick and his family for supper. Sometimes, they'd done so because Bethany and Josh begged her to stay. And other times, it was just more convenient for everyone. But this time, Fern suspected Nick's reasons were different. He'd had his most determined expression on his face when he'd left her to go get the *kinner*. When that heavy brow of his pinched deep in thought, Fern knew Nick hadn't given up. Knowing so gave her some hope to cling to.

Nick was a problem-solver. He may not have had an immediate answer to their problem, but he'd be working on one, no doubt. And Fern had an inkling that he wanted Ada present when he announced it.

In her heart, she couldn't believe *Gott* would take her from this family. Not now. And she prayed not ever.

"Where's Bethany going?" The woman's voice behind Fern was familiar.

"Ach, Rhoda. I didn't know you were here."

Fern spun around to face Nick's *mamm*, who stood in the doorway. Under her *kapp*, Rhoda Weaver's black hair was spun with silver-gray threads that matched the darkening clouds in the late afternoon sky around them, but her bright eyes held a sweetness that could calm any storm. Like Bethany, Rhoda was tall and slender with a gracefulness that matched the kind spirit she carried in all she did. She was the exact opposite of *Grossmammi* Beiler's petite but mighty steamroller personality. Fern and Charity had always been a little in awe of Rhoda Weaver.

Rhoda was still waiting patiently for Fern's answer.

"Oh, *ya*, Bethany went to see if *Gross-mammi* wants to have supper here tonight." Fern looked down at the pie, which was becoming humbler in size as the number of guests kept adding up. She'd have to make more if both of Nick's parents were staying for supper, "Is Daniel with you? Perhaps you both could join us, too."

Rhoda held the screen door open for Fern to pass. Josh had already galloped ahead in search of *Dawdi* Daniel. "Here, let me take that for you." Nick's *mamm* held the pie while Fern slipped her shoes off at the door. "I suppose Nick forgot we were coming tonight, but I've already set a chicken to stew and peeled potatoes and carrots, so there will be plenty enough to go around."

"Might as well make enough for Eli and Naaman, as well." Fern had a feeling a quiet supper was not on the menu for tonight.

"*Ya*, may as well be prepared." Rhoda didn't appear surprised at the mention of the bishop and her eldest son showing up. "And it's probably best to make enough for Ezekial and Leah, too."

Fern's *mamm* and *dat* were coming, too. Somehow. She wasn't surprised. And if Fern were to guess, she'd say the woman was well aware of the events coming to a head this day. And in her peaceful way, Rhoda was present to support her son and grandchildren through another rough passage.

As she followed behind the older woman to the kitchen, Fern's heart grew heavier. "Rhoda, I don't think I can bear to see the children suffer again. Or Nick. I know he won't suffer from my leaving as he has from the loss of Charity. But still…"

"*Nay*, there isn't any *but* about it. He'll be lost all over again without you." Nick's *mamm* straightened her shoulders and leaned a hip against the counter by the sink. She was looking Fern square in the eye. A glimmer of sadness was swiftly replaced with determination. "And the *kinner* will feel your absence strongly, Fern. Don't doubt for a moment that your absence will be anything short of a terrible upset to them."

"I feel like this is my fault. But I cannot change *Grossmammi*'s mind. I have tried."

"None of this is your fault." Rhoda picked up a large kitchen knife and chopped the peeled potatoes. "And Ada's mind is *not* the one that needs changing."

Some cryptic murmurings about Eli being their best hope followed before becoming further muffled by the rhythmic thwack of the metal blade against the wooden cutting board. Nick's *mamm* pushed the pile into a large pot of cold water, then paused and nodded at Fern. "You can cut up an onion real small. We'll add it to the potatoes for flavor."

So that was Rhoda's secret to the yummiest creamed potatoes in Promise.

Fern retrieved a knife and extra cutting board to help. Keeping her hands busy with the supper preparations gave Fern's mind a much-needed distraction from considering the actual meal and the fiasco sure to follow it.

In her hushed tones, Rhoda seemed to believe her eldest son was down at the store convincing Nick of his duty. But even Eli couldn't be persuasive enough to talk his brother out of a sacred promise.

If someone was going to have to break a promise, apparently the unspeakable was going to fall on Fern. With Ada and Rhoda both expecting Nick and Fern to marry, they had no hope of a solution that kept Fern here with the *kinner.*

Perhaps she might excuse herself along with Bethany and Josh after the meal before Nick explained to everyone that he would not marry

Fern. At least she'd miss the moment of her utter humiliation.

Although at this point, she wasn't sure which would be worse—for everyone to know a man wouldn't marry her even in the direst circumstances or that dire circumstances were the only means of convincing a man to marry her.

Chapter Three

After the last sale of the day, Nick retrieved his keys to close up. Turning the lock, he peered through the glass door as his last customer pulled out onto the road. He'd had a few hours to think things over and had hoped Eli and the bishop would show up sooner rather than later. Might as well get this over with.

Shortly afterward, a heavy knock summoned him to the back entrance of the store. Nick pushed against the swinging door that opened into a room used to unload deliveries and raised the loading dock door.

Eli, both taller and thinner than Nick, stood outside. Nick's senior by ten years, he appeared even older today. The worry lines etched deeply across his brow.

"Come in, *bruder.* I've been expecting you."

Nick looked closer out the back entrance. "Is the bishop with you?"

"I asked Naaman to let us resolve this as a family. He won't be coming."

Not this time. Not if Nick complied, Nick filled in the unspoken words. "We may as well get straight to the point, then. Naaman wants me to marry Fern Beiler."

Eli scratched his beard. "I've tried to send you hints this was coming."

Nick couldn't tell for sure if Eli was apologizing or annoyed with him. He took it as an apology. "I don't blame you, *bruder*. You're just doing your duty. But you also know very well why marriage is not an option for me— not until Bethany and Josh are older."

"I know you promised Charity not to let her children forget her. That was her worst fear because of what happened to her as a child. Ain't so?"

"*Ya.* That is the way of it." Nick's wife never knew her *mamm* and never understood her father's reasons for leaving her behind and remarrying in a hurry.

Eli set a hand on Nick's shoulder and looked directly at him as if by sheer will he could convince Nick of whatever he was about to say. "Fern and Charity were cousins, but as close as sisters. Ain't so? Who better than Fern to keep Charity's memory alive for her *kinner*?"

Unsure how to answer, Nick shrugged.

His brother stepped back, allowing Nick some space to consider it all.

Over the past few hours, Nick had thought on little else. Was Fern's love of his children enough reason to marry her? Fern's promise to Charity complicated the situation more than ever.

The almost-flirting from this morning came to mind. But he was no youngie who equated a heart-pounding moment for love. *Nay*, love— married love—required far more and from both sides.

Eli sighed. "So tell me truthfully, *bruder*. What is holding you back?"

"I appreciate Fern's loyalty to Charity and her love for the *kinner*. She's a faithful, honest woman. But Eli, you know as well as I do that... Fern is strong-willed." Although, at least she wasn't as stubborn as Ada. He couldn't imagine Fern pulling a stunt like this on a family member. "She is so different from Charity. I care about Fern, of course, in the way *Gott* would have us all love one another."

Eli raised an eyebrow. "Others see more in your relationship, but only you can judge your own heart. Still, you've always gotten along well with each other, and I've never noticed her strong will interfere with her care of your family over the past two years."

"*Nay*, Fern has been a *wunderbar* blessing. But we are friends. There is a difference, you know. And I don't think Fern would cross that barrier, even if I asked." He wasn't about to explain how he knew she was indeed that strong-willed.

Eli lifted his eyes heavenward, probably seeking divine help for this conversation bound to go in circles. "How will you know unless you ask? I think you may have to try. Even before Ada approached the bishop with her concern, he'd been praying over the matter. Her visit came to him as a sort of confirmation that it was time to step in."

"Because Ada is leaving Promise and taking Fern with her."

"Well, that adds some urgency to the matter, but it's not the heart of it." His brother tugged at his collar, appearing both uncomfortable yet gravely serious. "Ada's concern is for Fern. Her life is tied down to you without you being likewise committed. For the past two years, she's cared for your *kinner*. And you must be honest, for you also. You come home to a clean house, a hot meal, as well as contented children. How long do you expect Fern to put her own life on hold? Whether you and Fern marry is your own business. But I must agree with Ada. This arrangement is not a healthy one to continue indefinitely."

Put that way, Nick sounded like a real jerk. But he'd never sensed from Fern that she was unhappy. Of course, they'd all grieved for many months, but now Fern and the children seemed joyful again. She'd confirmed so herself that afternoon. And he was grateful to Fern for all she'd done to maintain a sense of normalcy in their home.

But if Nick married again, he'd expected it would be for the love and the companionship his heart ached for every lonely evening, every lonely buggy ride or walk to church, and every quiet holiday without his dear *frau* by his side.

Eli cleared his throat. "The choice is yours to make. As will be the responsibility of letting another mother figure Bethany and Josh love and depend on leave them, too." His brother nodded at him, as if satisfied Nick must understand the intended message

The menacing rumble of an early spring storm sounded in the distance like *Gott*'s punctuation to Eli's statement. Nick shuddered. The fatigue he'd carried since first light threatened to overcome him. But his day was far from over. Fern and Ada would both be at his table for supper.

The matter would have to be settled.

Heavy drops of rain pelted the tin roof as he prepared to leave. This had not been a good day to walk to work, and he was grateful when Eli also noticed the rain and offered him a ride home. Eli drove Nick home in his buggy but declined Nick's offer to stay. He'd said all he'd come to say and wanted to get home to his family before the storm worsened and full darkness fell.

"Besides—" Eli nodded toward two extra buggies parked in Nick's yard "—looks like you have plenty enough company for one night."

"*Ya*, it does," Nick agreed, noting that both his parents and Fern's had come for supper. His time had definitely run out. He had to figure out what to do—and fast.

As Nick exited his brother's buggy, the yellow-orange glow of lamplights turned on behind the living room and kitchen windows.

The welcome aroma of a chicken supper greeted him at the door.

He paused at the kitchen entrance. The fully

set table stretched in front of him. They'd been waiting on dinner for him.

His gaze landed on Fern first, but she didn't look his way. She sat at the corner of the table, next to his empty chair at the head. Her shoulders were straight and her hands folded in her lap with a stiffness that matched the air in the room.

Ada sat between Fern and her parents with Nick's *mamm* and *dat* seated on the other side of the table.

He'd interrupted something, he was sure.

"Sorry I'm late." No reason to explain. He could surmise easily enough everyone had already been informed about Eli's visit and its purpose. "I'll go get Bethany and Josh. I'm sure everyone is hungry."

Fern stood. "*Nay*, you go wash up. I'll get the *kinner*."

Ada clicked her tongue in disapproval. Fern's offer was motherly. Wifely.

And as Ada loved to remind them both, Fern was not his *frau*.

Fern ignored the reprimand and slipped past him without making eye contact.

Nick looked around the room from one adult to the next, seated at his table. He tried to tamp down his rising temper, but he'd had about enough. For all their efforts to guilt him into marrying Fern, she hadn't appeared this upset before. When it was only him and the *kinner*, Fern was fine. More than fine, she was happy. But the woman who just disappeared from the room seemed miserable.

And embarrassed.

"What have you said to her?" His glare landed on Ada, but he didn't wait for a response.

With long, purposeful strides, he followed Fern upstairs and overtook her just in front of Bethany's bedroom.

"Fern." He touched her arm so that she'd turn to face him. "Please look at me."

Her fingertips slipped to the corner of her *kapp* to hide her scar, wringing his heart like the twist ties he used to close bags of bulk goods at the store. He could do better for her this time.

He had to.

"What did she say to you, Fern? Something made you want to get away from that table." He had to assume this was more of Ada's doing.

"That's not why I wanted to leave. Nothing has changed since we spoke last. Well, except that Ada plans to leave in three weeks."

Three weeks. "So soon? Every time I talk to

you today, this matter just gets worse. What is happening?"

Her hand moved from the corner of her cap to twisting at the ribbon. He was making things worse. If feeling like his life was falling apart around him again was even possible.

"I'm not trying to make you nervous, Fern. I'm just not sure anymore what I am supposed to do to fix this."

Fern planted both hands on her hips and looked at him as if he were a hopeless case. "There is nothing left to do, Nick. You aren't making me nervous. I came up here because I don't want to be there when you tell them we aren't…that you don't want to…that this plan of Ada's isn't going to end as she thought."

He hadn't thought of that. "I don't really want to be there for that, either."

He waited for her to laugh.

She didn't.

"Sorry, Fern." Maybe he was a hopeless case. "But I don't understand Ada's sudden hurry. Has she spoken of this before?"

"*Nay,* not until today. I didn't see this coming, for sure and certain. Of course, she's hinted that we should marry before but… I don't understand this sudden move any more than you do."

He couldn't help but suspect there was more to Ada's new resolve than pushing him and Fern into marriage. "She is definitely going so soon?"

"She hired the moving truck and a driver as soon as I left this afternoon."

Ada had a reason for her actions. She always did. But in all his life, he'd never known Ada to be cruel. Outspoken and stubborn, *ya*. But she'd always loved Charity and Fern, maybe even favored them above her other grandchildren. So why would she do this to Fern and her own great-grandchildren?

Whatever the cause, Ada wasn't bluffing. But that didn't change the fact that Fern didn't belong anywhere else but right here in Promise.

"I won't let this happen—" He stuttered to a stop.

He didn't want to let her go. He wanted their lives to continue the way they were, but there was only one way to prevent his family from losing Fern.

"I'm afraid there's nothing we can do, Nick."

"We can marry."

Her eyes widened "*Nay*, you don't mean that." She shook her head.

"I do, Fern. We can't afford to continue to be stubborn about this. I don't want you to go.

And I can't bear to break Bethany and Josh's hearts."

She was too stunned to answer him, but she wasn't likely to back down. Like he'd tried to explain to his brother, Fern's mind was made up about him decades ago.

She was still shaking her head, as if she hadn't heard him right. But she hadn't actually said no, had she?

Suddenly, he felt as desperate to change her mind as Eli had been to convince him. That was it. He just had to repeat what Eli said.

"Think, Fern. This way you can keep your vow to Charity. That's what you want, isn't it?"

"What I want?" The puzzled look on her face suggested she hadn't much considered what she wanted.

He knew the one thing she didn't want—him as anything more than a friend.

"I won't expect you to be my wife in truth. But you belong with the *kinner*. And they with you. This is the best I can do for all of us. The closest way to keep our vows to Charity."

That was the reason behind this desperation pounding through his blood, wasn't it? To honor his promise. To treat Fern with the respect she deserved. To protect his children from another life-altering heartbreak.

So, it wasn't what he'd envisioned for the rest of his life. But those dreams of love and happiness had died once already. Maybe he'd never have them again, but at least he could bring joy to his *kinner* and protect a dear friend.

"Fern, if we marry, then we can simply go on as always." His conscience thumped him. Marriage was meant to be more. But the bishop had approved, hadn't he? "I'll do my best to make you happy."

If she'd agree.

Did Fern just hear Nick right?

His solution was for them to get married.

Fern shuddered as a boom of thunder overpowered them. Not that she had a response ready. She was at a loss without the heavenly interruption.

A flash of lightning sent Josh and Bethany running from the bedroom where they'd been playing. Josh raised his arms up to Bethany, begging for her to hold him. Too old to do the same, Bethany pressed herself against her *dat*'s long legs.

"It's only a spring squall. No need to worry." Nick ran his hand along his daughter's long loose hair. She'd taken off her *kapp* after school, a privilege she was still young enough to enjoy.

Slowly, Nick's gaze drifted from Bethany and back up to Fern. The plea in his eyes was as determined as it had been moments ago.

He was asking her to marry him. For the *kinner*. For Charity.

Until now, she hadn't felt her time spent with the *kinner* was any sacrifice at all. But to marry a man who wanted her as a wife in name only—a man who had been her friend as long as she could remember. Nick, who would never think of her in any romantic way, would be her husband.

Her stomach balled into a tight knot.

Josh's little head shifted on her shoulder and he looked up at her. They were all watching her. Waiting.

Clearly, the *kinner* overheard Nick's proposal—if the deal he'd offered could count as a marriage proposal.

"Puh-weeze?" Josh's arms wrapped tighter around her.

"We can be a real family. Wouldn't you like that, Fern?" Bethany added.

Her heart was as bound to these two as much as its every beat depended on the air she breathed. If she refused him, her heart would ache far worse than any disappointment over what this marriage might lack.

"Hush." Nick's reprimand lacked much conviction. After all, their pleas were in his favor. But his stormy blue eyes crashed into hers with a force that sent her heart soaring up into her throat. "It's Fern's choice to make and not an easy or fair one to ask of her."

Fern stretched her open hand to Bethany, who stepped straight to her side. Fern wrapped her free arm around the girl's shoulders. She squeezed both *kinner* with all the love her heart could spare.

Somehow, she couldn't make eye contact with Nick to give her answer. She looked at the children instead. "*Ya*, I would like that."

Nick moved closer, drawing them all into a circle with one hand on Josh's back and the other on Bethany's. "You mean you'll marry me?"

"For the *kinner. Ya*."

Nick winced. Or she imagined it, only because her own heart felt a pang of sadness. She'd never know the love she'd dreamed of receiving from a husband.

But then, she'd lost hope for love of that kind many years ago. Strange that today it would try to sneak back into her heart again.

Today, when she'd just sealed her fate.

Josh wriggled out of her grasp to bound down the stairs to the company waiting at the dinner table. His sister skipped right behind him.

"I doubt we'll be breaking the news ourselves." Nick nodded in the direction his *kinner* had just gone.

"That's for the best, I suppose."

"Fern, you can have some time to think about this. I shouldn't have pressured you like that. This is a big decision." He rubbed the back of his neck. The way he always did when he was troubled.

In reality the pressure had been building for months, even if her *grossmammi* had given them the final push toward the cliff. But his acceptance of the marriage ultimatum seemed to come out of nowhere. "Are you having second thoughts already, Nick?"

"What?" He shook his head. His hand came out as if he was going to take hers, but then his arm dropped back to his side. "*Nay*, I won't go back on my word. You know that. And I think we had our sign, didn't we? From *Gott* and the *kinner.*"

With a deep breath to settle her disappointment at a loveless marriage, she finally looked up at her friend.

He'd never go back on a promise given. She knew that, but she also knew it was his promise to Charity, not to her, that bound him to this marriage agreement. And it was her own promise to Charity that made her accept.

Plain and simple, this was their only choice. Nothing would change by waiting.

"We both have promises to keep," she finally answered with as much confidence as she could.

"*Ya*, we do." He gave a solemn nod.

Nick scratched his beard, then a half smile tipped one corner of his mouth. "The thunder and lightning came with perfect timing."

That was what he'd meant about a sign from *Gott*. He was joking to lighten the mood. He'd probably made other jokes that she'd missed, too. She attempted to smile back at him. "Those *kinner* have a way."

"They do." He fidgeted with his suspenders, as if unsure of what to do next. The volume from the rest of their family grew louder. "I suspect they've made the announcement for us. Everyone sounds pleased, for sure and certain. I suppose we should join them."

As she slipped by him to go downstairs, his

hand caught hers for a fraction of a second, and she looked over her shoulder.

"*Denki*, Fern." The sincerity of his words held her feet in place as she looked back at him—the man who would be her husband.

Nick was a loyal man and a loving father. And the sight of him in that moment was a picture she'd not soon forget—her sign that she'd made the right choice.

"I'll not go back on my promise, either, Nick." She watched the tension in his features dissolve into relief, then she headed down to the family that would soon be hers.

Fern couldn't recall the last time she'd seen so many cheerful faces around the table. Apparently, she and Nick were the only ones bearing the gravity of the decision they'd just made. For everyone else, it was a reason to celebrate.

But as Fern slipped into her seat, Daniel caught her eye. Was concern what she saw from Nick's *dat*? Or pity? *Nay*, it was not the *Poor Fern* expression she knew too well.

The fatherly attention didn't rest on her long, only enough to sense that Daniel saw below the surface of her smile as she accepted everyone's congratulations. *Ya*, he'd seen her resignation instead of the happiness she ought to have with an engagement announcement. But she hadn't had the chance to determine what her soon-to-be father-in-law thought about it.

She couldn't bear to look her own *mamm* and *dat* in the eye. Maybe this was what they wanted, but they wouldn't have forced her hand in any normal situation. *Nay*, if she looked at her *mamm*, she'd surely cry. They both might. Fern squirmed in her spot as they all bowed for silent prayer.

Three weeks.

In the middle of the reverent silence meant for prayer, the sudden realization disrupted her thoughts. If Eli and the bishop published Fern and Nick's engagement at this Sunday's church meeting, she'd be married in three weeks. The time Ada had given as their departure had now become her wedding date.

A shiver ran up her spine.

Nick cleared his throat to signal prayer had ended. She opened her eyes to find him watching her. His brow rose in question. She swallowed. Hard. Pushing this new panic aside, she passed the bowl of creamed potatoes to Nick and willed a peaceful smile to her lips.

She could do this. Life often changed in an instant. At least she had a bit of time to work this out in her heart and mind.

Fern passed the chicken pie.

"Aren't you going to take some?" Nick asked.

Her stomach churned in protest. "I'll get some when it comes back around. Let the others go first."

He frowned but took the dish without pressing her further.

She took a sip of water, hoping no one else noticed her empty plate.

Three weeks didn't seem nearly long enough to prepare for a lifetime as *Poor Fern*, the woman that handsome, likable Nick Weaver married out of pity for his *kinner*'s sake.

"Fern." Nick's voice was low, meant only for her. "It will all work out."

Setting down her glass, she nodded.

Fern wanted to believe those words. But all she could do now was her best and trust in *Gott* for the rest.

Chapter Four

Escaping the commotion of her wedding guests, Fern stepped out of her parents' home onto the back porch. Two hundred church members and extended family—aunts, uncles, siblings and cousins to both her and Nick— made for a smaller than usual Amish wedding, but more than plenty for her. Only she truly wished her brother, Martin, had been able to come. But bad weather had hindered travel up to the mountain for many, including Martin. She leaned her elbows on the railing of the simple wooden deck that overlooked her *dat*'s hayfields and the cresting slope of Promise Mountain.

A brisk breeze swept Fern's blue wedding dress tight around her legs as she rose onto her tiptoes for a clear view of the batter. After all, she was more than a little partial to this particular player.

The sound of a wooden bat cracked against the low pitch of a softball. Two stunned older Amish boys came to their senses and jumped the fence to chase the ball. But the hit deep into the neighbor's pastures earned an easy run all the way to third base—marked with a makeshift sandbag—and then a fast dash across home plate.

"That's my girl." A low whisper tickled the back of Fern's neck. She hadn't heard Nick join her, and her heart fluttered at his nearness.

She'd been fighting these weird sensations since the moment Nick had taken her hand that morning when they stood together in her father's barn for the wedding ceremony. Every time he accidentally brushed against her throughout the three-hour-long service, she'd barely contained the feelings that ran though her. Maybe it was nerves. Only what she'd felt was much more like pleasure than fear.

If she had any sense at all, she'd be afraid because this wasn't a young woman's dream wedding—the romantic kind. Her marriage to Nick was a sacrifice by two friends for those they loved the most in this world. Nick may not love her in a romantic way, but she was safe with Nick. She'd always known that.

Could he ever love her? She didn't want to replace Charity. No one could ever do that. But what if he found a place in his heart to love her as his wife, rather than his friend? Would she finally be free to love him back, as she hadn't dared since the accident?

So many questions. Ones she knew she should stop asking. They only led to a past she couldn't change and a future she would never know.

"Are you all right?" Nick moved beside her and was looking down at her with concern etched across his brow.

"*Ya.* I'm fine. You sounded a little too prideful, though." She didn't mean it, but she'd rather tease him than share the thoughts going through her mind and heart at that moment.

He pinned her with a look as if to say he knew she was as pleased by Bethany's home run as he was. She couldn't deny it.

Thankfully, all her thoughts weren't so transparent. She shivered at the idea of Nick knowing how this day had affected her.

"If you're cold, you should go back inside."

"I'm *all right*. I needed a break from the

commotion." Besides, she wasn't cold—not even close with his warmth so near.

"Here, then." Nick shrugged out of his coat and wrapped it around her shoulders. His hands stilled on the lapel, and his eyes met hers.

She couldn't breathe. The seconds ticked past with her caught in the memory of the last time he had draped his coat around her. He shook his head, as if clearing the same recollection from his mind.

"Fern, I'll do better this time. I promise." His hands dropped back to his side.

"Better than what?"

He shrugged and turned his attention back to the *youngies*' ball game. "I just mean that I intend to do right by you, better than I did in the past."

He'd saved her life that day with his quick thinking and his coat that had smothered the flames leaping up her sleeve and into her hair. The regret in his voice couldn't possibly refer to his actions that day—unless… Did he mean what had come next?

But he couldn't regret choosing Charity over her. He didn't. He wouldn't.

For sure, her tender heart had been wounded as much as her flesh had been burned and scarred, but she didn't want him to regret his choice. *Nay*, everything was as *Gott* had planned. It had to be. A world without Bethany and Josh was not a world *Gott* ever meant to exist.

Nay. Nick couldn't read her mind, and she certainly couldn't read his. He must have been thinking of something else entirely. He had to be.

With her eyes closed, she inhaled deeply. The scent of fresh-cut grass mixed with the warm chicken supper prepared in the kitchen behind her. Her lungs expanded as the mountain air comforted her from the inside out and she let out a slow breath.

Everything would go back to the way it should be after today. She and Nick and the *kinner* would return to their regular schedules. The hard part—the wedding day in front of so many people—was almost over. Life would go on as always. And all these irritating questions would go away.

Reassured, she opened her eyes and pushed back her shoulders.

Nick tugged at the sleeve of his coat hanging from her shoulder. "I'll return to our guests. Take as much time as you need out here."

"*Denki*, Nick, for understanding." She

slipped out of his coat and handed it to him, but he didn't take it.

"Keep it. I don't need it in that crowded house." He smiled and held her gaze for several heartbeats before leaving her outside— now feeling very alone.

But moments after he'd gone, she heard the back door open again. This time, it was her grandmother who'd come to find her.

Grossmammi was looking a little older and frailer, and Fern wondered how she'd not noticed the change sooner. She'd postponed her move until after the wedding, but the hectic weeks of wedding preparations and packing had taken a toll. As she approached, Fern sensed more behind the tired eyes. A sadness, maybe, and her heart squeezed with compassion.

Fern certainly hadn't wished to leave Promise. How much harder it must be for *Grossmammi*, even if she had pronounced the idea to be her own. Fern tucked her arm around her grandmother's elbow.

"*Kumm.* Sit here with me for a spell." Fern motioned to the porch swing.

Grossmammi patted Fern's hand as they rocked gently back and forth, and seemed as though she may take a nap right there until she broke the silence. "I believe you know Thomas Miller had a part in all this."

All Fern knew was that *Grossmammi* had received mail from her former son-in-law, Charity's father, and been unusually secretive and upset by it. "I don't know anything about Thomas or what he's up to really, but you can't mean he had a part in this marriage…" Scheme? Arrangement? Fern wasn't sure what to call it.

"For sure and certain, he did." *Grossmammi* thrust a foot onto the deck's wooden floor, bringing the swing to a halt. "It may not be a secret that I've long believed a marriage between you and Nick would be right for you both. But it is Thomas's greedy *frau* that pushed us to rush you and Nick to the same conclusion. Apparently, the rent I've paid all these many years on his property so that Charity, his own daughter, had a roof over her head is no longer enough. They want to sell, and I cannot afford the price they are asking."

"*Grossmammi!* I thought… We all thought that the property was yours. That you'd bought it from Thomas years ago."

"After your *aenti* Faith died and Thomas left their newborn *boppli*, Charity, with me, he arranged for me to live in the cottage there on his property and wanted the farm to go to Charity when she was of age. But as soon as he remarried, his new *frau* expected him to sell his land in Promise. To pacify her, he's collected rent from me for all these years with the understanding that the land was to be paid-in-full for Charity on her thirtieth birthday. But Charity didn't live to her thirtieth birthday. Still, I continued the payments believing the agreement still applied for Bethany's and Josh's sakes. I never told anyone. I didn't think the bishop would approve. But when Thomas went back on his word, I had to go to the bishop. So now, I've made a fine mess of what should be Bethany and Josh's inheritance. But at least Thomas is only selling the cottage. You and Nick and the *kinner* can still live in the farmhouse."

"Why didn't you tell me? I would've come up with something." But as soon as the words were out of her mouth, Fern knew the reason. *Grossmammi* wanted Fern settled and believed Thomas's greed had been providential to her wishes. But how very unfair. "Even if you want me married, you don't really want to go to live with Uncle Titus, do you?"

"*Ya*, I do. A move at my age may not be easy, but I only have so much time left. I did all I could for Charity. I've done my best for you, too." She pushed off her foot and the swing once again began to rock. "Nick will take care of you. And you will take care of the *kinner.* You don't need me anymore. What is life once we are no longer needed?"

"Oh, *Grossmammi.*" Fern blinked back the tears forming behind her eyes, and her grandmother clicked her tongue in a soft rebuke.

"None of that, now. This is *Gott*'s will for me. Don't you fret, there's a purpose for my time down in the valley." She patted Fern's knee. "Today is a day of celebration. *Ya?*"

"Ya." The expected response came out a little limp. If only she could release her heart to enjoy this day as freely as a new bride should. But she'd be deceiving herself and bound for disappointment to wish this day held the same meaning as it did for a couple deeply in love.

"Gut," *Grossmammi* stated, as if some great matter was settled. "It is time for the marriage supper—to take your place at the table with your groom. And please, *Liebling*, put a smile on your face."

A commotion of cheers and activity pulled Fern's attention back to the yard to see the girls' softball team celebrating a win. Bethany skipped onto the porch. Her eyes were bright and her smile brimming with delight.

"Did you see? We won. We beat the boys!"

Fern ignored the click of her grandmother's tongue, undoubtedly meant to caution Bethany against bragging. But if a smile was what *Grossmammi* wanted, then this was how she'd get one from Fern. Bethany's joy spilled over, and the worries weighing on Fern's heart were forgotten in the moment.

"Wunderbar!" She pulled Bethany into an embrace. "Your *dat* saw your home run, too." Fern smiled down at her stepdaughter.

Her stepdaughter. Fern was a mother.

She looked over the top of Bethany's head and caught her grandmother's gaze. *"Ya, Grossmammi."* This time, her words held conviction. "I have many reasons to celebrate."

The moon was high in the sky now, full with a hazy ring, a sign of snow on a night this cold.

"There you are." Nick spoke tenderly to his mare as he gave her a sugar cube. "It's been a long day for us all, hasn't it, girl? But we'll be home soon and tomorrow you can spend all day out in the pasture."

A long line of horses with their buggies had been tied along the fence rails leading up to Fern's family home for the wedding festivities. He knew this place well, after all he and Fern had grown up as neighbors. Her *mamm* and *dat*'s farm was directly beside his own parents' farmhouse. As *kinner*, he and Fern had rarely been much more than a stone's throw away from each other.

And now, they were guaranteed to remain closer than ever.

His mare, Sadie Mae, was the last horse remaining along the fence rail. Nick untied her and slid into the buggy to drive up to the house, where Fern was waiting.

Everyone was drop-dead tired after all the events of the day. His *mamm* had already taken Bethany and Josh to her house for the night. He and Fern had offered to stay with the Beilers, the custom of most newlyweds, so they could help put everything back to right around the place in the morning. But Ezekiel and Leah, Fern's parents, insisted that almost everything was done already and fretted over the chance of snow.

Fern was probably as suspicious as he was, but neither he nor Fern argued. What was the use, except to make things more awkward than they already were. And they'd already decided that Fern would stay in Josh's room—his son barely slept in it anyway.

Something else was bothering Fern, though.

He just couldn't figure out exactly what it was. Of course, she'd have any number of reasons— this being their wedding day. He'd done everything he could to put her at ease, but he'd started to think he was the actual problem. He still wasn't sure whether she'd shivered from the cold or because his nearness made her skin crawl.

He'd never considered that he'd need to earn Fern's trust. They'd been friends for as long as both of them could remember—a friendship that had survived through the awkward teen years, his marriage and even their mutual loss of Charity. Maybe he'd been naive to believe that today wouldn't change things between them.

But something had definitely shifted, and he didn't think he was going to like it. Not if she kept turning cold whenever he was near her. The vows they'd exchanged bound them together for a lifetime. And even if this marriage wasn't a love match, he'd taken comfort in the fact that they shared a special and lasting bond.

But instead of being comfortable in that friendship and the way this arrangement had worked out, Fern seemed perfectly miserable. And he had no idea what to do about it. At least supper had gone better, without much of the tension that had been present during the service that morning. Fern had smiled and relaxed at the table beside him, easing his guilt, if only a little.

Sadie Mae nickered at him, displeased with his inattention. The horse was right. He needed to focus. He was likely just tired and overreacting. A good night's rest would set everything back to how it was before. *Ya*, he was sure of it.

He hurried up and drove Sadie Mae to the front door of the Beilers' house and pulled on the reins to bring her to a stop. He had one foot out the door to go help Fern into the other side, but she didn't wait for him. Before he could get both feet on the ground, she was opening the door on the other side. He swung his legs back around and shut the door to keep out the cool night air.

Fern's side door clicked shut and the fabric of her dress rustled against the seat as she scooted back.

"You ready? It's crisp out there tonight. Do you need a blanket?" Nick offered.

"*Nee*, but *denki*, just the same. I'll be all right. It's not far to…home." The last word squeaked through her lips. Her shyness pinched at his heart.

"Fern, I don't want you to feel awkward at the house. You haven't before, have you? I mean, our home has always been as much yours as—" As what? Charity's? Had he truly been so close to replacing Charity with Fern? "As much as any of ours. And now, even more so, *ya*?" Nick did his best to cover his own sudden hesitancy. They had to get past this horrible awkwardness somehow.

A light flurry of snow swirled in front of them. He kept his focus on the road but sensed Fern studying him. She'd barely dared to look at him all day, but now she was sizing him up. She had a knack for that—figuring out what was going on in his mind.

"I am trying as hard as you are, Nick, to act like usual. But you must admit that this just isn't. Besides, I've never been married. And I never thought it would be like this if I was." She paused, and he snuck a glance in her direction. Her shoulders slumped, making him wonder how many troubles weighted the burden she carried. "We don't need to pretend, though. Everyone knows. I heard them today, whether they meant for me to hear them or not. And they are right. Charity was your great love. I cannot replace her."

"Fern…"

"*Nay*, do not try to cover it up for my sake. I do not wish to replace her. I loved her, too, you know."

"I—I know, of course. I'd never think otherwise." And he couldn't help what was true, but must people be so cruel? "I am sorry that I cannot offer you what you want. What you deserve. But I want you to be happy, Fern. I do care for you that much." He always had. And he'd always come short of being what Fern really wanted.

She swiped a hand across her cheek and cleared her throat. "We are both tired, Nick. A good rest is what we need. All will look new in the morning."

"*Ya*, that is what I think, too. It's been a long day." And their whole purpose in today was to maintain life as usual. "Tomorrow will be better."

"I hope so." She didn't sound as positive as he'd like, but it was better than nothing.

They settled into silent contemplation until Nick turned up the lane toward the house. Fern leaned forward, straining to see out the front.

"Is someone at *Grossmammi*'s? Eli gave her a ride home over an hour ago. But there's a van in the drive and the porch light is on." Concern laced her voice. She leaned back and turned her head in Nick's direction. "Can we stop? I just need to make sure she is all right."

"Of course." The snow was picking up, but it didn't matter. Besides, the house was just across the way. He wasn't sure why she even asked when he was already steering the buggy to the side of the road. "I'll take Sadie Mae up to the barn and be right back over."

She nodded and was out the side door in a flash.

Nick wiped the sleeve of his jacket across the condensation on his door window. Exhaust filled the air behind the van idling in Ada's driveway, and an Amish man stood in her doorway. He couldn't see Ada, but assumed she was on the other side. Taking in the situation, he decided he should tie Sadie Mae here and see what was happening right away, instead of taking the time to go to his barn and return.

He jogged across the yard and caught up to Fern at the bottom of the steps, just as the Amish man turned around to see them. He hadn't seen or heard from Thomas Miller since Charity's funeral, and before that, he'd only ever seen her father on their wedding day. Seemed the man had a knack for remaining scarce except for weddings and funerals.

"You're a little late for the wedding, Thomas." Nick trudged up to the top step behind Fern. "What can we do for you?"

Before the man could answer, Fern reached around the imposing figure of Nick's former father-in-law and pulled on the screen door handle. "Why don't we go inside to talk? It's freezing out here and starting to snow."

"No need." Thomas held up a hand. "Seems I missed Ada's message that you'd all be held up another week before moving. My driver is waiting. I have family in Roanoke to visit. But I'll be back in a few days to go over the final details."

Nick had no clue what the man was talking about, but one thing was for sure, this was not a night to be driving down the mountain to the city. "Thomas, those roads are going to get slick in a hurry." Nick couldn't help but hesitate. Inviting Thomas Miller into his home on his wedding night wasn't an easy thing, but what choice did he have? "You can stay with us."

"I've already failed at talking good sense into the man." Ada stepped out on the landing beside Fern. "I offered him to stay here tonight, but he's made up his mind."

Nick looked from Ada to Fern, who tugged

at her *kapp* string. But she wasn't just nervous, not the way her eyes narrowed, with a gaze strong enough to melt Thomas into a puddle right then and there. Nick guessed she knew something more than he did about this situation. But it wasn't like Fern to keep secrets. Unless Ada had asked her to.

Thomas moved closer to the steps. "Ada's right. I appreciate the offer, but I'll be on my way. I'll be back, though. The buyer interested in the farm is anxious to see it in person. As I told Ada, I've held him off as long as I can without losing the sale." He nodded at each of them in turn and scurried down the steps and off toward the waiting van.

Nick couldn't make any sense out of it. "What farm is he talking about?" he asked Ada.

Ada shyly slipped back behind the screen door.

"*Grossmammi.* This afternoon you said he still owned and wanted to sell the *dawdi* house, your cottage, but you didn't mention anything about selling the whole farm. What is going on?" Fern's narrowed gaze was pinned on her grandmother, while Nick remained frozen in stunned silence.

Ada sighed heavily. "He's talking about your farm, Nick. It wasn't exactly Charity's inheritance, although I felt truthful in explaining it to her that way because I always intended it to be hers. I rented it all these years, along with this *dawdi* house, so she could have a home. We had a rent-to-own agreement—a verbal understanding. Thomas never gave me the deed, but rightfully, the land was to be mine. At least, that's what I thought, and I planned all along to leave it to Charity when I passed." Ada paused, looking first at him, then at Fern. "Of course, I would have left it to both of you. But Thomas's heart changed after Charity died. Or at least, his wife was able to change his mind. They want to sell it all to someone else."

"But earlier you only mentioned this cottage, not the land and farmhouse, too." Fern sounded as puzzled as Nick felt.

"He only ever mentioned intending to sell the *dawdi* house before now. But his wife has a cousin who invests in real estate, and she has other plans. Apparently, this man has deep pockets and now Thomas wants to sell both, and he still has the deed to all of it. That's what he came here to tell me. He has that real estate agent coming to look at the place in a couple days."

The numbness of Nick's shock began to thaw with the heat of something very much like outrage. "You could have said something sooner, Ada. I would have done my best to help." Instead, she'd manipulated the situation to suit her plans for him and Fern to marry. But that wasn't even the worst of it. How could Thomas do this? Even if the law wouldn't stop him, what about the church? "If he gave his word to you, we might appeal to his bishop."

"I—I tried." Ada's voice broke. "I went to Naaman for help, but his appeals to Thomas fell on deaf ears. And the bishop in Thomas's district was not willing to become involved. There doesn't seem to be anyone to stop him."

Slender fingers cupped around Nick's hand, and he looked down as Fern glanced up at him. "But *Gott* can. He will make a way."

She squeezed his hand and let go—the momentary touch replaced his rising indignation with a sense of relief. Whatever had caused Fern to pull away from him earlier, she was here now. Her steadfast, solid friendship—his rock in times of trouble—hadn't disappeared, as he feared.

He released a long, slow breath. Tomorrow wasn't going to be business as usual, after all. But he couldn't process all this news after the day he'd already had. He didn't have much hope of getting any sleep now, either. But he'd have time to think. To plan. There was a solution to this problem somewhere, and he would find it.

Ada's head hung low. "I'm so sorry."

Apologies from Ada were rare, for sure. And Nick felt uncharacteristically sympathetic toward her. Maybe when he'd had more time to consider everything, this revelation would shed new light on the woman and her ways.

"You cannot take all the blame, Ada. But we are all too weary to talk more tonight." He nodded at Fern. "We should go."

Fern kissed her grandmother good-night, and they made their way back to the buggy.

Nick knew Fern was right. *Gott* would not let them down. Although at the moment, he didn't know how much lower he could go. No matter how hard he'd tried since Charity died, his world kept shifting out from under him.

Chapter Five

As far as Nick could see from his bedroom window, the mountainside was covered in a heavy blanket of snow. If the height of the mound on the edge of the barn roof was an indicator, somewhere between eighteen inches and two feet had fallen during the night. He'd finally fallen asleep after mentally rehashing the events of the previous day and the implications of Thomas and Ada's revelations. And the muted silence that always resulted from a big snow had kept him blissfully unaware of the sunrise. He couldn't remember the last time he'd slept so late.

The peace seemed deceptive when he thought about all the challenges ahead of him. Or perhaps *Gott* had graciously given him extra time to adjust by slowing the world down to a stop. All business would be on hold up here in the mountains today. Even if the expected warmer temperature melted the snow in a hurry, the back roads were bound to be impassable for most folks for a day or two.

Unless...

A smile ticked up at the corners of his mouth. Unless you had a horse and a sleigh. In three long strides, he reached the bedroom door and swung it wide open.

"Fern!" He called loud enough for her to hear from downstairs, maybe even all the way outside.

"Fern." He tried not to yell this time, but his excitement was hard to contain. He galloped down the steps in search of her.

"What is it?" Her voice called to him from above, where she stood in her nightgown. Her hands rubbed at her eyes.

"It snowed." He sounded like a child. And his enthusiasm from a minute ago felt silly. "I'm sorry I woke you."

He looked down at his bare feet. He hadn't even finished dressing. His suspenders and socks remained upstairs. He ran a hand through his hair. He was a mess, for sure. "I just assumed I was the only one who slept so late."

He looked back up, suddenly struck by the

fact Fern's hair was loose and uncovered. His heart stuttered. He hadn't seen her hair down since they were children. Silky as warm honey, it hung down to her waist.

Seeming to read his thoughts, she retreated a few steps. "I'll be right down," she called from somewhere out of sight.

Suddenly embarrassed by the thick, curly mop on his own head, Nick bounded back up the steps to the washroom to make himself more presentable. And when he returned downstairs, Fern was already in the kitchen, stoking the fire in the woodstove for breakfast.

She'd tucked her hair neatly under her *kapp* and puttered around the kitchen like it was any other day.

"I'll go do Bethany's chores. The poor cow must be miserable by now." While he was in the barn, he could ready the sleigh. "I thought we could take the sleigh out. That's why I was looking for you. What do you think? We can go pick up the *kinner* and take them for a ride."

She closed the door on the stove and looked up at him. Her eyes sparkled. "I think they'd love that. I would, too."

Nick felt his earlier excitement return. He edged toward the mudroom door. "I'd better get a move on, then, before the snow turns to slush."

Fern began opening up cabinets in search of something, then pulled out two large thermoses. "I'll make hot cocoa and gather up their winter coats and mittens. It will be *wunderbar* fun, Nick."

Both he and Fern made quick work of chores, even digging Fern's cabbage and broccoli plants out from under the snow. Even if they had to leave them behind and move off the farm, she couldn't bear to see them go to waste. Nick wasn't convinced the plants would survive. But Fern was pleased, and she was a far better gardener than he could ever be.

Soon enough, they were on their way to his parents' house. Sadie Mae's hoofs cut a rhythm with each step through the icy crusted top layer of snow while the sleigh's runners below maintained a steady swoosh as the rest of the world remained in silent reverence of the wonder of nature's surprise. The white landscape was pristine, only marked with the occasional trail of deer or small animal tracks.

Along the wood line, a bushy-tailed squirrel stood at attention to watch them pass. Nick glanced at Fern, snuggled under the blanket and watching the scenery go by. An impulse struck him to bypass his parents' house and take a ride along the mountain ridge. And even though horses weren't permitted on the Blue Ridge Parkway, there was a lesser-traveled back road that would suit his purpose even better.

They'd pass almost every Amish farm in the district, and the snow-covered mountain road would be perfect for the sled, and the views spectacular.

When he veered right instead of left, Fern gave him a look as if he'd momentarily forgotten what he was doing. "Where are you going?"

"Maybe couples who just got married a day ago ought to spend time together—without their *kinner.*" Her wide-eyed shock matched his own at what he'd just said, but he laughed to give himself a second to consider why exactly he'd said such a thing. The answer wasn't hard. He'd spent a good portion of the night pondering on the matter.

"Fern, I can't help what people say. And I cannot change our circumstance to be a different one. But I can be careful not to give the gossip too much fuel." He suddenly determined to take the long route close to the Blue Ridge Parkway. Let a few folks see them out together alone this morning. "Besides, neither of us gets many days off. *Gott* has given us this one, so we can enjoy it. *Ya?* Imagine how beautiful the Blue Ridge will be in this snow." He leaned over and wiggled his brow, as if inviting her to join in some childish mischief. "Wouldn't you like to take a ride and see?"

She burst into laughter, confirming he appeared ridiculous in any attempt at flirtation. Of course, he wasn't flirting. Not really.

"It would be, *ya*. I'd like to see it very much." Her mittened hand slipped out from under the blanket and rested on his shoulder. "*Denki*, Nick. It's very thoughtful and kind of you—considering what others might say."

One heartbeat. Two. A very slow third and she put her hand back under the cover. Nick's throat went dry. Maybe he wasn't such a bad flirt after all.

He had only meant to protect Fern's heart from mean gossip. Apparently, he needed to take more caution to spare himself, as well. He knew for sure and certain Fern would never react to him in the hopeful way his own heart had just betrayed him.

He was going to have to be more careful about a lot of things.

Nick's detour was unexpected, and Fern wasn't sure what to make of it at first. And the way he'd stared at her this morning, as if seeing her for the very first time. Her heart sped up at the memory. She'd been able to recover quick enough, once she'd ducked out of sight, by telling herself she must have imagined his admiration.

But had she? When he'd wanted to take out the sleigh with her—alone—she'd dared to wonder.

But then, his mannerisms brought back memories of the old Nick—before the burdens he carried now—when he'd invite her along on some childish adventure. Catching crawdads in the creek after a rough day of school or gathering bushels of black walnuts to sell at the farmers co-op after getting in trouble with his *dat*. That's how Nick handled stress. It only made sense that with the predicament Thomas had created for them, a peaceful ride was a very Nick-like way to cope with a looming tough decision. Not a romantic honeymoon gesture—she'd shoved that fastball of a notion as far out of reach as one of Bethany's home runs.

The scenery this morning was breathtaking. Almost enough to forget Thomas's visit last night. The sights of the past half hour had kept them in conversation.

They talked about things that they hadn't had time to discuss the past few hectic weeks. Maybe Bethany would benefit from some time with her cousin Cassie, learning to bake and decorate cakes. Was Josh doing enough chores for his age? Fern wondered if she was spoiling him a tad in that area. It was a good thing the local apple trees hadn't bloomed before this snow. Sadly, the fruit trees in the lower elevations might be ruined.

And then there were the comfortable quiet spaces between words, simply enjoying nature as the sleigh carried them through bend after winding bend in the road. Only now Nick had turned around to head back, and each new observation began to feel like a forced way to avoid the subject looming ahead of them.

As they eased around the turn off the Parkway to return to Promise, Fern noticed Nick's shoulders square off. He felt it, too. Like it or not, they'd soon have to face the inevitable.

If word hadn't reached Nick's parents already, they'd have to tell them. She may as well be the one to broach the subject. "Do you think word will get to your *mamm* and *dat* ahead of us this morning?"

"Always possible, I reckon." His voice held a hint of disapproval. "I wouldn't be surprised to find someone has already gotten to them, even on a day like this."

Fern wouldn't, either, which was why she'd wondered, of course. "In this case, it might make it easier. Then we won't have to do all the explaining."

"That's one way of looking at it, I reckon. But I'd rather be the one in charge of my own life. Seems like everyone had an idea of what was going on except for you and me. And I don't want to ruin a perfectly fine morning, Fern, but it's not right."

Thomas's deception was a terrible shock and a great wrong to her grandmother. Nick had to have seen that Thomas took advantage of *Grossmammi*. The man had gone too far in his greed. Surely, even his bishop would see the need to talk reason into him now.

Some pieces of the puzzle that had plagued her for weeks about their families' behaviors had fallen into place last night. She was upset, too, but understood a little more what had caused their families to push for the marriage.

"I don't believe anyone really knew what Thomas was up to, Nick. At least, not his full intentions. Thomas sprung that last part of selling the farm on *Grossmammi*, too."

"*Ya*, well, maybe she'll know how it feels for

once. Keeping secrets and manipulating people into doing what she wants. Thomas took a play right out of her book."

That stung,

Fern felt manipulated into this marriage, too, but his words cut like a double-edged knife. No wonder he'd been hesitant to talk about it. He'd been simmering like a pot about to boil, and she'd turned up the heat.

She knew he had a reason to be angry, but it wasn't like Nick to be so unfair. Selling the cottage out from under her grandmother was cruel enough, but the entire farm! She didn't deserve the blame for that. Almost thirty years of rent ought to have paid for the place in full. *Grossmammi* had kept an awfully big secret, but not an all-so-bad one.

Fern's spine stiffened. "You might recall the secret she kept was that she was buying the farm to give to you."

Her words came out more defensive than she'd intended and were likely to add even more fuel to the fire.

Nick turned to face her; his eyes rounded, but he didn't respond right away. Instead, he looked back at the road. After a moment his rigid shoulders slumped. "You're right, Fern.

I'm sorry. I guess it's going to take some time to see Ada in this new light."

Fern blew out a pent-up breath. "I understand. Old opinions die hard."

He gave her a questioning look but didn't ask whatever was on his mind.

"What?" Curiosity got the better of her, even though she ought to let it go rather than risk another disagreement.

"It's just something I've been wondering... how to change opinions. I mean, if you want to change someone else's opinion about you. A very old opinion, that is. One you are sure the person will never feel differently about."

Thankful for a new subject, she relaxed back in the seat.

"I don't know." She wished she did. For instance, how did one change the mind of a husband who felt trapped in a marriage? She'd wondered more than once over the past few weeks whether Nick's mind about her might ever change. But he couldn't know that. He had to be referring to his own opinion about Ada. "I guess, in this case at least, it's having knowledge about a person you never understood before that is changing your opinion."

"Hmm." He rubbed his beard and chin.

"But when you've known a person your whole life…"

"I suppose we might think we know everything about a person and still be wrong, after all." Everyone had some secrets they held secure in their own heart. Fern did. And she'd made sure no one ever knew.

"Seems so, doesn't it?" The look he gave her was so piercing she feared he'd see right through to her thoughts.

She squirmed under the scrutiny and looked down at her feet. She shouldn't feel bashful with Nick. But then, she'd been experiencing more new feelings around him lately than her usual ones.

"I didn't think this would be so awkward. Did you?" Still focused on the floor of the sleigh, she swallowed hard. "I mean, we've known each other forever. And we have a routine. And I just hoped…"

"To keep everything the same?"

"Ya." She aimed a cautious sideways glance in his direction. "But it's not so easy to speak my mind. Before, we were always in familiar territory. But this is not. Not at all."

Nick reined his horse to a slow stop on the side of the road, then turned to give Fern his full attention. "There is a lot we cannot change about our marriage—the way it all came about, for one. But we can choose how we go forward. Whatever this day, or the next, throws our way...whether it's Thomas or any number of other troubles, we have to be free to talk to each other." He placed her hand gently in his, as he'd done for their vows the day before. "I won't keep anything hidden or secret from you. I promise. And I want you to feel safe, always, to tell me anything that is troubling you."

The same shiver she'd experienced at the wedding ceremony trilled up her spine. But this time, she didn't pull away from him. She met his gaze.

"*Denki*, Nick." She ought to say something more. Only how was she to repeat his promise back to him? She wasn't sure she could tell him absolutely everything.

He nodded at her, smiled and then urged the horse back onto the road. The kindness of the fact that she wasn't automatically expected to return the promise made her heart swell.

Nick was a good man. No secrets. No lies. That she could do. But she wasn't about to tell him how drastically being his wife was affecting her heart.

"I've been thinking." Nick spoke once the sleigh was fully back on the road and the horse going at a steady pace. "The only way I could buy the farm from Thomas would be to sell the store. But I'm not likely to make a living on farming." He gave a wry chuckle. It was true. Nick was a great shopkeeper but when it came to farming, he was barely Amish. Everyone had always teased him about it. "What do you think about adding onto the store? I know there's not much room out back, not at ground level, but a second level could also go above the store, which would make almost as much square footage as the farmhouse. Of course, I have to price it all out and see what I can afford, but it's the best option I've been able to think of so far."

"I think…oh my…it's a *wunderbar* idea." She shouldn't be surprised he'd come up with such a smart idea so fast. "You always have a plan, Nick, but I didn't imagine you'd have such a *gut* one already."

"Don't give me too much credit, Fern. Sure, this will give us all a roof over our heads, and that's enough to be thankful for, but what about all the memories we'll be leaving behind? The whole reason we married in the first place was to honor our promises to Charity. How are we supposed to keep her memory alive when we leave everything about her behind?" A vein twitched along Nick's temple and his grip on the reins turned his fingers white. She'd never seen him fight with his emotions as much as he'd had to do today. He was usually full of solutions with no patience for dwelling on the negative.

Had he finally hit a wall? It wasn't like Nick to let trouble get the best of him. Her heart ached for him. He was confiding his worst fears to her, as a husband would. And if she was a real wife, she'd know how to bring him comfort.

How she hated feeling so inadequate. As the church women had whispered yesterday, she wasn't Nick's great love match.

But they were matched—for better or for worse.

She might need to keep any romantic notions to herself, but she wasn't ready to quit. Not this easy. And not because of Thomas Miller. If *Grossmammi* had fought against the consequences of Thomas's selfish choices all these many years, then now was not the time to give in.

"Nick, listen to me. *Grossmammi* never let Thomas Miller's poor decisions ruin Charity's life. And we won't let him ruin her memory, either. I don't know how we'll do it, but I didn't get married yesterday to keep a promise only to give up today. And I won't let you, either."

He didn't respond.

She sucked in a deep breath, waiting.

She knew for sure and certain Charity would never have spoken to him in such a way. Fern could never be her cousin—not for Nick, not for anyone—no matter how hard she might try. She hadn't ever attempted and wasn't going to start now.

Nick had never rebuked Fern's forthrightness—not as her friend. Would he now that she was his wife?

"*Denki*, Fern." He said at last, with no hint of annoyance or censure. "I needed to hear that."

Keeping his thoughts somewhere far out of Fern's reach, Nick drove silently down the familiar road to his parents' house. Not so far she couldn't guess at them. She was sure he yearned for Charity—a wife with a soft touch and gentle ways to soothe him.

She didn't dare try to comfort him with a touch. She bit her lip in frustration, as well as to hold back the tears threatening to spill over. Would she always feel so inadequate in her role as Nick's wife?

Nick's gloved hand found hers and squeezed her mittened fingers. "Please don't cry, Fern.

I'll find a way for you to be happy. *Gott* will take care of us."

As his hand slipped away to return to the reins, she watched the man who was always her friend, always her protector. She should be satisfied. She wanted to be.

Why did her traitorous heart have to keep yearning for more?

Chapter Six

A steady stream of customers kept the bell over the entrance to Weaver's Amish Store jingling. The rush was to be expected on a Saturday like this one. In the weeks since Nick's wedding, beautiful weather and spring blooms painted the Blue Ridge Mountains in splendid colors and brought curious travelers to the area.

News about Thomas Miller's dealings had traveled faster than Nick expected. The whole of Promise's church district agreed Thomas Miller should be brought to task over the way he'd swindled Ada. But since Thomas belonged to a different district, there was no consensus on what could be done about it. And while Nick appreciated the concern of others, he also knew the whispering and unrest made Fern miserable.

Their marriage had set sail in choppy seas, and he was desperate to steer them into calmer waters. Fern had never liked to be the center of attention. This added conflict only made it harder for her. So rather than draw out a lengthy resolution between two Amish communities, which was likely to go absolutely nowhere in the end, Nick felt the sensible and compassionate thing to do for Fern's sake was to move forward with building living quarters onto the store.

As planned, Ada had already gone to live with her youngest son. Fern's parents, Ezekiel and Leah, helped her move and were still away visiting with their kinfolk. Nick, Fern and the *kinner* moved in with his *mamm* and *dat* as a temporary solution until the construction on the store was finished.

To his knowledge, the farm hadn't actually sold yet. Still, he was out from under any obligation to Thomas Miller by moving. And clearly, Fern was much relieved now that she no longer had to deal with Realtors or potential buyers stopping by the farm.

All in all, he supposed things had gone as well as possible. And yet, a persistent unease churned in his middle like sour milk. Something was off. Not something—he knew what it was—his marriage. As well intentioned as he and Fern had been, they hadn't solved the problem of keeping Charity's memory alive— not now that the home with all her memories had been left behind.

Nick pushed his pencil behind his ear for safekeeping as he moved to the next aisle of the store. He worked around customers, so as not to disturb their shopping, and was almost finished making note of the items that needed to be restocked.

He scanned over the jam and jelly section and noted several items that already needed to be replenished. His *dat* had even stopped in today to help. The church *youngies* he employed part-time were busy running the deli and the checkout, so his father came in to restock the shelves.

Nick slipped out of sight behind the last aisle and headed to the storeroom.

"How's it going?" His *dat* stacked a box on top of a loaded hand truck, then paused for Nick's response.

"No sign of slowing down anytime soon." Nick placed his notes for restocking on top of the box his father had set down. "As you can tell by this list."

"Well, I'd say that's a good problem to have."

His *dat* chuckled as he read Nick's shorthand. "You made the right choice to keep the store rather than the farm. I've always said you got the Amish business genes from your *mamm*'s side instead of the Weavers' farming ones."

Nick didn't bother to explain how that old joke had lost its charm years ago.

"Fern, she has a way with growing things. She's still tending the garden she planted this spring at the farm. It's a shame someone else will get her harvest, if the place sells quick enough. But she sure isn't going to let those plants die." His *dat* was shaking his head, but Nick knew his father was inwardly proud of Fern's talent and refusal to quit on the garden she'd kept growing each year since Charity passed.

Nick's regret that Fern would have to give up her garden was an added loss to all they were leaving behind on the farm. "There won't be room here for much gardening, other than the flower beds."

"She's welcome to a garden space in my fields if she'd like to plant a vegetable garden."

"Denki, Dat." Fern would appreciate the offer. Not only did she have a green thumb, but she loved preserving homegrown vegeta-

bles and fruits. Almost as much as he loved eating them.

"And make sure you add plenty of windows for her flowers." His *dat* laughed. Fern was using every sunny spot in the house for the plants she'd rescued from Ada's little greenhouse. Then, his *dat* pointed toward the inside of the store and frowned. "Not sure I have a solution for the ruckus out there. That kind of noise will travel right up to the addition you're putting overhead. Ain't something a woman will appreciate if she's got babies trying to sleep."

Nick shook his head. Where had that idea come from? *"Dat..."*

"I know more than you think I know, *sohn*." His father's voice was gentle yet firm. "And it appears I still know a far sight more than you, if you believe you can love that woman from a distance for the rest of your days. You're only fooling yourself. Take my advice and look for a way to soundproof that space while you do your planning."

Nick knew better than to argue, even if he was sure that such a thing would never be necessary. Not for him. Not for Fern, which bothered him more than any sacrifice he'd made for this marriage. He had his *kinner*, his work, his reputation.

Suddenly, he felt sick over how much it cost Fern to marry him, especially since nothing was turning out the way it was supposed to. Their lives were meant to keep going as always, but nothing was the same at all now. Fern had given up any chance at all for children of her own, and rather than being respected for her sacrifice, she was pitied.

Poor Fern. He knew she hated that phrase. He was growing to despise it, too.

"What's holding you back, Nick?" His *dat* shook his head. "I have to tell you I never thought you to be this stubborn."

Nick sighed. "I think you know who the stubborn one is. And it's not me."

His father chuckled.

"I'm not joking, *Dat*. Everything was easy with Charity…until she was gone." Nick swallowed to keep his voice steady. "Fern is different. She loves the *kinner* with her every breath. But me… She won't let me in." Especially not now, given the fact that everyone seemed to pity Fern for being stuck as Charity's replacement. "I don't think that's ever going to change."

His *dat*'s expression grew solemn. "That'll

be your loss, son. A strong-minded woman is a treasure for a man who learns to love her right."

Nick had heard a few tales of his parents' courtship. His *mamm* had set her heart on another man before meeting his *dat*, and winning her over had been a challenge. Nick had always taken the story as a good reason to pick a girl who was actually interested in him.

"*Mamm*, you mean?"

"*Ya*. You may not have inherited my farming talents, but you can't be so very different from me in this. If I could win your mother's heart and keep her happy for over forty years, then you can win over Fern, for sure and certain." His *dat* waved Nick's note. "I can handle this. Maybe you should check on things outside."

It only took a second to catch his *dat*'s meaning. Fern had mentioned she hoped to plant flowers at the entrance today.

"*Ya*, I could use some fresh air," Nick conceded with no idea how he'd fix anything with Fern but he'd enjoy her company, as he always had.

He ducked out the back door and gulped in several deep breaths of fresh mountain air. The scent of redbud and rhododendron filled his senses. The familiarity of his place in the world steadied him.

A soft hum fluctuated on the breeze. The rise and fall of the song notes grew louder as he approached the side of the building and headed around to the front.

He saw her then, squatted down with a trowel in hand and surrounded by trays of healthy young plants. She'd nurtured the flowers herself from seeds in Ada's small greenhouse before taking them to his parents' place.

She hadn't noticed him yet, clearly in deep concentration. He stayed back so as not to disturb her as she plotted out her design. She'd shown him her plan on paper days ago, and now she was setting each colorful bloom in its spot by design. By early summer the corner entrance to the store would be blanketed with a perfect quilt of flowers.

His *dat* made a valid point. How long could Nick continue this way? Not only was it getting harder to keep his promise to Charity, he didn't know how he was going to keep his promise to Fern. He was doing the best he could to make her happy, but he'd also promised things would go on as they always had.

Always friends. He knew she'd understood his meaning, and it was the only reason she'd agreed to marry him. But more and more, he wished he'd never restricted them to walk such a narrow path.

He'd been afraid she'd refuse his proposal because she felt nothing more for him than the friendship they'd always known. And if he was honest, he'd been afraid to hope for more—to try for more. It wasn't just the rejection he'd felt from her after her accident that held him at bay. After all, they'd been barely more than children. And now that he'd suffered a tragedy of his own, he realized a teenaged girl suffering as Fern had been with her burns couldn't be blamed for being oblivious to his feelings for her back then. Her rejection hadn't been personal, and he wasn't fool enough to hold such a petty grudge.

Maybe his *dat* was right. Fern wasn't the issue. Nick was.

Fern liked to give him credit for being a problem solver when he really just had a knack for finding the easiest solution.

Loving Charity had been easy. When Fern withdrew from him—from everyone—after the fire, Charity had been there for him. She was a simple, eager-to-please, impossible-not-to-love girl who became a *wunderbar* wife, mother and companion. He'd made an easy choice in loving Charity.

Loving Fern had been, well, complicated. And now, complicated had become mighty near impossible.

She was a treasure, a rare one. He knew that. Appreciating a good-hearted woman like Fern came natural enough, unless a man was a total blockhead. But loving a strong-minded and intelligent woman like his *dat* loved his *mamm* was another thing altogether. A powerful love required understanding a woman's needs, opinions and feelings. With Fern, that required a deeper effort of both mind and heart than he'd understood as a young man. And certainly more than he'd had to expend with Charity.

Sure, he was more mature and experienced, but was that enough? And even if he loved Fern in the way she deserved, would it be enough to convince her to take a chance at loving him back?

He had his doubts. And if he failed and somehow ruined the fragile but workable life they were making, then he'd have to live with the consequences for the rest of his life.

But if he succeeded... Well, his *dat* was right on that point. Loving and being loved by Fern would bring a lifetime of happiness, the kind that few ever enjoyed.

He suddenly realized Fern's humming had stopped.

"Nick?" She had twisted around to see him. With one hand holding a flower against her knee and the other with the trowel resting against her hip, she looked puzzled before she pushed up to stand. "What are you doing over there?"

Staring. Dreaming. Wishing for what he'd never have.

"Just came out for a breath of fresh air." That was true enough. "It's been a busy morning."

She bent over to lay the last flower in the ground, then walked over to meet him where he still stood beside the store. "You've been standing here for ages."

He cleared his throat, embarrassed that he'd been caught watching her. "Your design—did it work out like you hoped?"

She pushed a loose strand of hair back under her prayer *kapp*. "I think so. Want to see?" He nodded, then held out his hand to take hers as they walked down toward the sign and flowers. She glanced at his extended hand.

"What?" she asked, as if the gesture confused her.

"The trowel," he murmured, desperate to hide his embarrassment. "I can help for a bit to give your back and knees a rest from crouching down on the ground." Of course, he'd meant to hold her hand as they walked over to see her work, but he accepted the digging tool instead. A poor substitute but a mighty quick save, he inwardly congratulated himself.

A teasing glint reflected in her eyes as she released the trowel into his hand, confirming she knew exactly what his intention had really been.

Ya, he was going to have to work hard if he was going to win over her affections. When he caught a hint of laughter from her as she walked ahead of him, he knew the challenge was on.

This time, he intended to win.

Fern didn't expect Nick to dig holes for her flowers for very long. For one thing, she enjoyed the task. She'd tended these plants carefully from seedlings and wanted the satisfaction of finishing the job. And besides, she knew Nick couldn't leave his nephew, Zach, in charge of the front of the store much longer. Of course, Amish *youngies* knew how to work, but some supervision was always a good idea. Pretty Merry Yoder was working at the deli counter, and everyone knew Zach Weaver would flirt given any opportunity.

A family trait today, apparently.

She tried to hold back, but a laugh bubbled out from her. Whatever was on Nick's mind, he was acting very odd. She thought about his promise to share everything with her. She could ask what had him standing by the side of the store so transfixed, but she was a little afraid to find out.

Things between them had settled into a delicate balance since they'd settled down with her in-laws, Rhoda and Dan. Things had become easier with the establishment of a new routine and the constant presence of family around them. Nick's parents and her own knew she and Nick didn't have a true marriage. And since no one was trying to pretend any different, she almost felt as if they'd gone back to how things were when they'd been friends growing up. For the most part, at least. Sometimes one of their family members still attempted little matchmaking tricks, like leaving them alone on the porch together or taking the *kinner* out to give them some time alone. But for the most part, their schemes were perfectly harmless.

Still, keeping her emotions in line was

something like balancing on the ridgepole of a barn roof. Reading too much into Nick's occasional flirting would throw her off-balance for sure. *Ya*, it was much safer to forget the way her heart had fluttered when he'd attempted to hold her hand.

Nick stepped beside her and surveyed the plants she'd lain out in a Scandinavian star pattern. Not all the flowers had bloomed yet, so she'd carefully labeled their colors to ensure the design would appear exactly as planned when all the flowers came into full bloom.

"It's going to be beautiful, Fern."

"*Denki*. I hope so."

"Of course it will. This is the third year you've done this. You know we get tourists who stop for no other reason than to see your 'flower quilts.'" He walked gingerly around the edges, careful not to disturb the plants or freshly tilled soil, rubbing at his bearded chin the whole time. He acted like this when he was solving a problem.

"Is something the matter? You can tell me."

"What?" He spun around to face her. "You mean with the flowers? Nay, of course not. I was trying to figure a way to make room for a greenhouse in the construction plans. I'm afraid it would have to be very small."

She sucked in a breath. He couldn't have surprised her more.

"Oh, Nick, that's very thoughtful, and more than I ever expected." Letting *Grossmammi*'s greenhouse go had been a disappointment. She'd grown flowers with her since she was younger than Charity. And with the loss of the farm, too, she'd wondered how she was to continue any kind of gardening at all. "I've considered another option. Well, I never considered that you'd build a greenhouse. But... What about a nice sunroom? The back entrance to the house will have to be long and narrow, and it will also get the morning sunlight." The real living quarters would be upstairs above the shop, so a sunroom at the entrance wouldn't take away living space. Of course, it would need to be practical to be worth the expense. "It could also double as a mudroom on one end."

"That's a *wunderbar gut* idea." Nick smiled down at her and rested his hands on her shoulders, making her heart beat wildly in her chest. A feeling she didn't recognize buzzed between them as his gaze searched deeply, pondering some silent question she couldn't quite decipher.

"Later," he said as his hands skimmed down her arms to take hold of her hands, "we'll go over the plans and you can tell me exactly how you'd like for it to be. I want this new home to suit you, Fern. You deserve at least that much."

The depth of his caring warmed her more than the sun, now high overhead, and yet she was a little shaken. If she allowed herself to feel all that seemed hidden within his gaze and his touch, her heart would cross the boundaries their friendship had long held in place. And that friendship was the sure footing keeping their pretense of a marriage in place.

The tenderness in his eyes made her mouth go dry, and she couldn't find a response. He gave her hands a gentle squeeze, then walked away, leaving her unsure exactly what had just changed between them—only certain something new had begun—and she was losing her grip on the feelings she tried so hard to hold back.

Chapter Seven

Another week almost gone, and the building project felt stalled. Standing outside the store's front entrance, daylight ebbing into sunset over the mountains, Nick posted a Closed sign onto the door. The warm May weather and the clear skies promised to hold through the rest of the week, but tomorrow was to be a special day for family and fun.

The Amish didn't work on Ascension Day. But even locals would forget that he closed his store every year on this particular Thursday. So he taped a simple reminder—Closed for Ascension Day—onto the front window, locked the door and descended the steps.

Nick could hear his brother, Eli, and his niece Cassie talking as he rounded the corner to retrieve his bicycle. So much had changed in the weeks since his wedding, like how he no longer lived close enough to walk home from work. Not to mention that his home didn't exactly exist at the moment.

As far as he could tell, he was the only one chafing at being back under his parents' roof. Everyone else seemed perfectly content, but he was making no progress at all with Fern, surrounded as they were with family all the time. Instead of a marriage, their relationship felt more like they'd gone back to their childhood when Fern was at the Weavers' house as much as she was at her own home next door.

Somehow, that bothered him. Sure, he'd been the one to propose this sham of a marriage, but leaving the farm behind and moving in with his parents wasn't exactly what he'd expected. So, he spent every spare minute getting ready for the construction of their new home.

Eli waved at him from beside his wagon, filled with supplies from the local feed and seed co-op. Cassie waited inside the rig, while her *dat* strode toward Nick. "We're headed your way, if you'd like to ride with us."

"*Denki*, Eli." Nick tossed the bike in the back and climbed up beside his niece. He preferred taking the bike to work rather than leave

Sadie Mae hitched up all day waiting for him. Still, the ride from his brother was appreciated.

"How are the house plans coming along?" Eli asked.

"Truth is, adding a second story to the current building is more complicated than I expected." And more expensive. He was coming to realize they might be living with his parents longer than he'd hoped. "I'm still waiting to hear from the architect."

"No doubt you'll have plenty of help when the time comes for the walls and roof to be raised. It may not be a barn, but you know the district will gather to help, as always, when the time comes."

"*Ya*, that I know and am thankful for it."

"Um…" Cassie squirmed beside him, removing a basket from the seat between her and Eli. "About that…" She clung to the oversize bundle, likely filled with goodies for tomorrow's festivities. She shook her head. "Never mind."

"Might as well be out with it, *dochter*." Eli chuckled. "Whatever it is, you won't be able to hold it in long."

"Well, I heard some talk among customers today while I was making their sandwiches." Cassie glanced at Nick out of the corner of her eye, then turned to her *dat*. "It may be gossip. You wouldn't want that."

"Don't you know if it's gossip or not? If so, you ought to have put it out of your mind as soon as you heard it." Eli's reprimand was half tease. Cassie was anything but a gossip.

The poor girl rubbed at her temples. "It's nothing bad about anyone. But it's hearsay. I mean, I can't know if it's true." Again, she looked at Nick for a brief moment, then back to her *dat*. "If it is true, then I think Nick and Fern ought to know."

"Cassie…" Eli's patience seemed to thin as he drew out her name and rolled his hand as though she needed to get on with it.

"I heard that the developer Thomas brought up here, you know, his wife's non-Amish cousin, well, he got wind of what happened to Ada and is threatening to pull out of the deal. Not because he cares, but it's bad for business." She bit at her lip. "That last part might be gossip." She shifted in her spot again, as though the basket weighed a hundred pounds. His niece was such a tenderhearted girl—young woman now. He'd never heard her speak a bad word of a single soul. "I mean, we cannot judge whether the man cares or not, after all. But this seemed important. Everyone wishes the land would remain Amish, with farmland being so scarce and all. I thought maybe…"

"*Denki*, Cassie, for telling me." Nick hoped to ease her mind. She did the right thing to tell them, but it wouldn't make any difference for his family. The price Thomas was asking for the farm was well beyond his reach.

When the day had come for him to leave the home that held all the memories of his life with Charity, he'd grieved. Deeply. And in his grief, he'd been comforted by a sense that God was moving him away from the past to a new future. Saying goodbye to his home had been too difficult to allow himself to hope for a different outcome now.

Thankfully, Eli changed the subject to the family plans for the following day, which Cassie was more than happy to chatter about until they reached the Weaver farm. And Nick was relieved not to talk any further about Thomas Miller or losing the farm that held all his *kinner*'s memories of their *mamm*.

"Will you tell Fern?" Eli spoke in a low tone to Nick after Cassie had jumped out and gone ahead into the house.

An odd sort of question, Nick thought. "We aren't in the habit of keeping secrets. Why do you ask?"

Eli shook his head as he tied up his horse near the watering trough. "I wasn't implying any such thing, not intentionally. Just seems this kind of news would affect you more than you are letting on. And Fern, too. I had to wonder what she'd make of it. Folks are certain to believe this is a chance to keep the farm in Amish hands, but no one will want to make a move on it without your blessing."

"*Ya*, I see your point." Nick scratched at his beard. He'd have thought of that already, if he hadn't been quite so surprised by the news. Every time he thought his life was moving forward, something happened that made him reconsider all the choices he'd been forced to make over the past couple of months. "I suppose the news did affect me strongly, as you said. I'm just tired of it all. When's a man allowed to move on?"

Eli's arm came around Nick's back and his hand clapped Nick on the shoulder with a brotherly squeeze. "I'll take care of this mess with Thomas from here on out. You've enough to worry about. Now, let's go enjoy the blessings of the family *Gott* has given us. Tomorrow there will be no work...*and* no talk of land sales or troublesome outsiders."

"*Denki, bruder.*" A weight lifted from

Nick's shoulders, and he felt lighter as he stowed his bike in the shed.

As he turned to head inside, Fern appeared on the porch. She was waving them inside. "Supper's ready!"

When he came near the porch, her smile widened. She must've had a good day.

He smiled back.

Would he tell her? Eli's question echoed back to him. Of course he would. After the holiday, though, just in case the news might trouble her. She'd planned a special picnic for him and the *kinner* tomorrow, and he wasn't about to ruin it.

Breakfast around the Weavers' large table held a crowd on Ascension Day morning. Bethany and Josh's younger cousins had spent the night at their grandparents' house, making a full dozen young *kinner* in the house. Even though the Weavers' other older *grosskinner* hadn't stayed over, Cassie had spent the night to help with all the children. She hadn't seemed to mind at all, because she'd also loved the tradition when she was younger and got to sleep over.

Nick and his *dat* had herded the gang outside to play while Rhoda, Cassie and Fern cleaned up. The silence was a blessed relief. No wonder Nick had winked at her as he'd passed through on his way out.

Cassie washed the last plate and stood staring out the window at the children playing. "Remember, Fern, how you would come over from next door and play with us?" Cassie asked as she handed Fern the dish to dry. "Back then, you and Nick would play games with us outside. It's strange to think I am older now than you were then. You were the big kids in school, and I wasn't even old enough to go to school yet, but Martin…"

Fern's hands stilled with a tea towel in one hand and the wet plate in the other, at the mention of her younger brother, Martin, wondering which memory of him Cassie had cut short. Since Fern's brother had left their community, folks rarely mentioned Martin. He'd never joined the church, so he wasn't shunned. But he never wrote or came to visit. Fern missed him terribly. Apparently, she wasn't the only one. Cassie's eye glistened with unshed tears.

"You were always so kind to Martin. *Denki* for that, Cassie." Martin hadn't been like the other children. He'd struggled to fit in, but Cassie had always been friendly to him.

Cassie simply nodded and excused herself,

leaving Fern and Rhoda alone in the kitchen, undoubtedly not for long as busy as the house was today. Rhoda took the now-dry plate from Fern and placed it in the cabinet. "Is she all right?" Fern asked her mother-in-law.

"Time will tell." Rhoda's brow pulled together. "Although it has already been a few years since he left, and they were closer than you may think. Still, I don't know what any of us can do about it."

If Fern knew of a way to bring her brother back, she would for sure. But she had no idea what they could do, either. Besides, she knew Eli would never allow a romance between his daughter and Martin. She'd often wondered if that was the reason Martin left in the first place.

"But we can do something about today." Rhoda's eyes brightened and the lines across her forehead had disappeared. "In fact, I've already assembled your picnic basket for you. I see no reason you and Nick can't go enjoy the rest of the morning and your lunch together away from this noisy bunch." She smiled knowingly at Fern and handed her the packed basket, which felt considerably lighter than she'd expected.

"Oh well, there's no rush. The children are having such fun. I'd hate to take them away so soon." Fern lifted the lid of the basket. Two sandwiches, two drinks, two cookies. Fern felt her mouth drop open in confusion.

"Who said anything about the *kinner*?" Rhoda shrugged. "Now go on. Zach is coming any minute now to help Cassie with his little cousins. You and Nick can scoot. It's a day for family time. And you and Nick have some work to do in that department."

Fern felt the heat of a blush travel up her neck. How utterly humiliating. What would Nick think when she waltzed up to him and said they were going on this picnic—alone—after she'd made such a fuss about how much she was looking forward to it?

"Rhoda, you know that this marriage is not like that. We haven't made it a secret that we are still only friends."

She could hear the panic rising in her voice, but Rhoda didn't budge. "I'm sure Daniel has explained the situation. Now go on. Everything will be just fine. Trust me."

Oh, that was asking for a lot, even from Rhoda.

Nick stepped into the kitchen then, drawing Fern's attention away from Rhoda. He was as red-faced as she felt. Exactly what had Daniel explained?

Looking at the basket looped through her arm, then back up to her face, Nick cleared his throat and pasted on a smile. "Ready?"

She didn't need to ask for what. Clearly, he'd been pressured into this, but at least he knew it wasn't her idea.

She'd thought taking the *kinner* to the old farm for a picnic would be nice. No one was living there, and Thomas Miller would never make a fuss over a picnic after all the trouble he'd caused them. They could lay a blanket to eat and even play ball with Bethany. Nick knew she'd done so for the *kinner* for a chance to make a memory and share a story about their *mamm*. The idea seemed to please Nick, maybe even relieve him, since leaving all their memories behind had grieved him so.

"They mean well." His voice held a hint of apology as they walked through the back door. "We can stick to your plan if you'd like or go somewhere else."

"I don't know." This sudden change threw her off-balance. "I can't think of what else we might do."

"There's that horse trail up along the old railroad. We can take the back way to avoid the road and picnic along the way. Today would be perfect for it. If you don't mind riding horseback, Sugar is in the barn. Your *dat* won't be needing her today." His face lit with a good-humored smile.

The Weavers were caring for her parents' horse while they were gone to help *Grossmammi* settle in her new home and visit with *Onkel* Titus. Her *dat* wouldn't mind even if he was at home, and Sugar was used to trail riding. Sadie Mae wasn't as comfortable with a saddle, but she would cooperate for Nick.

"I don't mind. I've always enjoyed riding Sugar, and maybe it's for the best to do something different." His shoulders relaxed with her agreement. Apparently, he didn't much like the idea of revisiting old memories, at least not without the *kinner.*

She followed him to the barn to saddle up the horses and wondered if he might do her a favor. "Do you suppose we could swing by the farm, just for a minute? I was going to pick the last of the sugar peas to go with lunch." Of course, there was plenty to eat in the basket. It wasn't really necessary. "I just don't want them to go to waste."

She'd planted the garden before the wedding. Unlike her flower seedlings from *Grossmammi*'s little greenhouse, she couldn't dig up a vegetable garden and carry it with her to the

Weavers'. Now, the garden was going to go to ruin. She could hardly stand the thought.

As they crossed the threshold of the barn, the sweet smell of corn and grain mixed with the sharp tickle of hay and straw. She walked toward the horse stall, but Nick stopped her with a gentle hand on her arm.

"We can go wherever you like, Fern. We can stay if you prefer. And if you'd like me to stand up to my meddling parents, we can do exactly as you planned and take the *kinner* with us."

Her heart swelled. Not because she wanted to picnic at the farm, but more at the thought that he was willing to stand up to his parents for her sake, even if she didn't need him to do any such thing. His idea to go up to the Blue Ridge Parkway was growing on her.

"*Nay*, Nick, maybe we do need a little time alone, just the two of us." After all, they hadn't had a chance since he surprised her with the sleigh ride almost six weeks ago. "If you don't mind."

"I've never minded being with you." He'd moved so close to her now that she could see the flecks of green in his blue eyes. "Especially on Ascension Day."

A flood of memories raced through her mind. She'd always ended up at the Weavers' on this special day, instead of with her own family, because Nick always asked her to come.

She shivered and her hand flew to the scar under her left ear. The warmth of Nick's fingers wrapped around hers and drew her hand away from the scar that warmed beneath his touch.

She couldn't decipher the emotions at war on his face. Only one other time in her life had she wondered if Nick might kiss her. They'd been here in this very barn, and she hadn't known what to do. Still didn't.

"I know you're in there!" Bethany's voice rang out just before she ran into the barn.

Fern jumped, and Nick took a broad step to the side.

"Oh, it's you." Bethany's mouth formed a pout. "We can't find the twins. Have you seen them?"

Fern shook her head.

"*Nay.* If they're in here, they're hiding *well*. But I wasn't looking for them, either." He winked at Fern and went about getting Sadie Mae ready for the buggy.

She looked at the picnic basket still hanging on her arm. That wasn't going to travel well on horseback.

"I'll just go put our lunch in a backpack."

Fern edged out of the barn, willing her heart to cease pounding, and wondering how much she'd just imagined. Probably as much as she'd imagined the first time. Nothing came of it then, and nothing would still.

She ought to remember that.

Chapter Eight

Nick had been absolutely right. The day was perfect for trail riding. Fern's worries narrowed down to the pleasurable task of guiding Sugar as they followed Nick and Sadie Mae. Flowering rhododendron and azaleas marked the sides of the wide path left behind from an old rail line, long defunct and grown over with moss and grass.

Sugar's ears perked back, her focus steady and her gait smooth along this fairly flat stretch. Her horse could do this all day, but she'd need a drink soon, and Nick was already aiming for a mountain spring not far ahead.

Fern couldn't help but wonder what might have happened in the barn if Bethany hadn't interrupted—or if she hadn't been caught so off guard. She'd pushed the memory of their long-ago almost-kiss far from her mind ever since her cousin had fallen in love with Nick. But as she rocked along the trail to Sugar's easy gait, she'd barely been able to keep it from her thoughts.

The memory had changed with age. She recalled things she hadn't understood as a sixteen-year-old. Back then, she'd assumed Nick had pulled away because her scar had repulsed him. On further reflection, she recognized his actions in a new light because now she'd witnessed the same expressions from him when he was protecting his family.

Could it be so simple as that he hadn't wanted to hurt her?

Her heart lurched forward along with her body as Sugar came to a sudden halt.

"Easy there." Nick soothed the horse. "Didn't you see my signal that I was stopping?"

Fern shook her head. *Nay*, her focus had been somewhere else entirely, which she wasn't about to admit to Nick. Fortunately, he didn't question any further.

"I know the spring is nearby, but it will be easier for me to find on foot." He slipped down from his saddle and came around to Fern, holding out a hand to help her down.

Thankful she'd thought to slip a pair of leggings under her dress for modesty and warmth while riding, she swung down beside him. The strength of his grip eased her landing, but he didn't release her hand even after she was safely on solid ground.

She wondered how Nick meant for them to walk the horses on the uneven forest floor and continue to hold hands, but she didn't let go. Neither did he. If anything, he gripped tighter, and still managed the task until they came upon the rock where fresh water bubbled from the mountain. They let the horses loose to drink.

With a long upward stride, Nick climbed onto the rocky ledge, then pulled Fern up beside him so they could sit with their knees bent over the edge. The ground where the horses rested was only a foot or so below their feet, and the moss-covered rock face behind them made for a comfortable seat.

"Are you thirsty?" She nodded in reply, and he removed the backpack from his shoulders.

"Nick?" She'd taken a few sips from her water bottle, and he was reaching for the sugar snap peas they'd stopped to pick from the garden. He popped one in his mouth, then turned his face toward her. He raised his eyebrow, waiting for the rest of her question, only it had hung up in her throat.

Did she really want to know what happened all those years ago? She wasn't sure where the answers would lead. But the tenderness in Nick's eyes this morning in the barn, the mention of their long-ago inseparableness, the protective touch of his hand around hers as they walked and the completely comfortable way they could sit so close to one another made her wonder how much she'd misjudged.

"Fern." He swallowed, set the bag aside and wiped his palms along his thighs. Then his forefinger came to her chin, warm and gentle, redirecting her focus back to his face. "You can talk to me about anything. It's okay."

"Why didn't you kiss me?" The boldness of her question startled her. Her face heated red the instant the words were out. But Nick refused to let her look away.

His mouth turned up in a half grin. "I think you know."

Nay, she didn't. But he tipped his head closer and appeared dangerously close to doing it now. She leaned back. "No, not this morning. I mean, back then…after the accident…before Charity."

Nick leaned his head back against the mossy rock and blew out a long breath.

Fern fidgeted, worrying the lid of her water

bottle with her fingers. The length of the silence made her stomach sick. Those memories were so painful, even still. Tears threatened behind her eyes, but then the warmth of Nick's hand loosened her now-fierce grip on the edge of the rocky ledge between them.

"I wanted to," he said simply, contradicting everything she'd believed. Surely, she couldn't have been so wrong about it all for all these years.

Nick knew he had to be honest. For a brief second he considered a casual response, something like, of course he'd wanted to kiss her back then. He was a guy, and she was a pretty girl. But his conscience prodded him not to take the coward's way out. Not this time.

Fern was scooting to the edge of the ledge. Her feet touched the ground, and she stood. "But you didn't. Why? Were you afraid you'd hurt me?"

"Not exactly." He wished he could say it was. He wouldn't seem so daft, might even sound honorable. But he'd had the excuse of being a kid—no longer a valid justification for running from his fears. And she was pinching the bottom corner of her prayer *kapp*, tugging it down over her scar.

"It's hardly noticeable anymore, you know. You don't have to cover it." He pushed off the ledge to stand in front of her. "You never had to cover it with me."

"I thought the scar made me repulsive, ugly. All this time, that's what I thought." Her voice was soft, almost as if she was talking more to herself than to him.

"*Nay*, Fern." His voice cracked and a part of his heart along with it. He reached for her hand, and she let him take it. He rubbed his thumb across her knuckles. "I promise I never thought so.

"That day I pulled you out from the fire, I realized that I never wanted anything bad to happen to you again. I was too young to know how impossible that was. Life has thrown us a lot of curveballs since then. But when I wrapped my coat around you to smother those flames, I wanted to keep you cocooned forever." Her hand was ever so still in his, and she looked back up at him. Her eyes were wide and the trail of a tear meandered down her cheek. He swallowed at the lump forming in his throat.

For the next two years, he'd tried. But in the end, he wasn't good enough. "I didn't kiss you that day in the barn because I thought you needed someone else. Someone who could make you happy again. Because you were so desperately unhappy, and I couldn't seem to do anything about it." He let go of her hand and kicked at a clod of dirt. "But that man never came, and now you are stuck with me."

She pinched at the bridge of her nose and sniffed. Digging around in the backpack, he found a napkin for her to blow her nose.

"Charity used to say that."

"What did Charity say?" His late wife didn't know anything about how he'd felt about Fern. He didn't court Charity for well over a year after he'd let go of the idea of a life with Fern.

Fern tucked the napkin into her sleeve. "That a man would come…who'd love me for who I was…the way you loved her." She swiped at her wet cheeks.

On impulse, he pulled her into his arms, tucking her head beneath his chin. He held her there, close to his heart to keep her from witnessing the agony sure to show on his face. Charity wanted more for her dearest cousin than this sham of a marriage. More than he might ever live up to.

Fern released a shuddering breath into his chest, then pushed back. "She wanted me to be happy. And, Nick, she'd want you to be happy now, too. Maybe it can't be like what you had before, but we can do our best to make each other happy." She squeezed his hand before letting it go. "Today—" she motioned all around them "—is a *wunderbar* start."

Sugar came and nuzzled her hand as it fell back to her side. She grasped at the reins. "We should keep going."

"Ya." His heart could only take so much at once. The ride back down the mountain would give them both time to absorb all they'd revealed to each other.

He swung the backpack over his shoulders and took Sadie Mae's lead. They hadn't eaten, but he'd find another spot to picnic, maybe along the roadside meadows. He led the way back to the main trail, where he helped Fern back into the saddle. The old sense of protectiveness he'd had for her resurfaced as she carefully placed her foot into his hands. Once she was in the saddle, Fern smiled down at him as if to say she was all right. He didn't have to worry.

He gave her a nod but stopped short of a smile. He stroked Sugar's neck before mounting his own horse. They hadn't solved anything. And once again, he had that old feeling that Charity would know what to do.

She'd want you to be happy, too.

He glanced over his shoulder at Fern. She was ready, so he signaled Sadie Mae forward.

As he replayed Fern's words in his head, he realized Fern wasn't quite right about what Charity had said. Happiness wasn't what Charity wished for Fern. *Nay*, she wanted Fern to be loved.

Promise me.

How was he supposed to keep his promise to Charity and love Fern in the way Charity had wanted for her cousin at the same time? He doubted she ever imagined the task would fall to Nick. But it had.

He wasn't sorry for it, just doubtful Fern had ever wished for him to be the man to answer that need.

Except maybe for one thing. Fern had wanted him to kiss her. If he'd been sure of that back then, his life—their lives—may have taken a very different path. But *Gott* hadn't seen fit to give him that understanding back then. Now that he was aware, he looked forward to finding out where the knowledge would lead.

She'd wanted him once. Could he make her want him again?

As long as he stayed true to his promise to Charity—as long as their children remembered their *mamm*—maybe there'd be no harm in pursuing Fern. And there might be a lot of joy.

* * *

Fern's stomach rumbled. She hadn't felt like eating when Nick offered to stop in a nice pasture on Sam Yoder's farm. And she hadn't been ready for a long stop with nothing to do but talk—or worse—sit in silence with the awkwardness of their earlier conversation between them.

I wanted to.

Something inside her began to heal when Nick said those words. Not that she could figure how it changed much of their current circumstance, but the thought of that long-ago day no longer felt sore when she recalled it.

Could she dare hope that Nick might love her? He chose to build a home for them rather than sell the store and stay at the farm. Of course, that was a sensible business decision, and yet his plans included designs meant just for her. Wishing for love still seemed overly optimistic, but not as impossible as it had just this morning.

She could settle for happy. Or so she'd hoped when she'd tried to comfort Nick earlier. The agony of the position he'd been put in had been apparent in the way he'd held her. An involuntary shudder ran up her spine. She'd never wanted anything more than she'd wanted to ease his pain in that moment.

Her stomach growled louder, and she regretted the choice to keep going. She was starving, for one. And Rhoda was sure to question why they'd returned with all their food.

The old home was close, so she urged Sugar up alongside Nick to suggest stopping there. Funny, they were going to end up back where they'd originally planned to go all along. Although this would only be a quick stop.

Rather than set out a whole picnic, they settled on the front steps and tucked into their sandwiches. Nick's whole sandwich disappeared in three or four bites, so she pulled out the bag of pretzels for him.

"Denki." He smiled at her. "I was getting famished."

Before she could respond, the crunch of automobile tires caught their attention as an all-black sedan eased into the drive. As the vehicle came to a stop, she recognized her *dat* in the passenger seat, then her *mamm* in the back. Her uncle lived near Beachy Amish, who drove all-black vehicles with no radios or special features. Her parents must have hired one of them to drive them back to Promise after they got *Grossmammi* settled at *Onkel* Titus's.

The driver was the first to get out of the car. All she caught of his face was that he was young and unshaven, and though she couldn't see all of his clothing, he wore suspenders, making her assume he was most likely an un-married Beachy Amish man. He turned to close the door, revealing his face.

"Martin!" The sight of her little brother had Fern running across the yard so fast, she wasn't positive her feet had even touched the ground.

She came to a sudden stop right in front of him, remembering just in time that Martin had never been fond of loud noises or the kind of hug she desperately wished to wrap tightly around him now.

He was grinning at her. His light brown curly hair was windblown. And his brown eyes actually met hers for more than a brief second, making the moment feel even more special since he'd never liked eye contact much, either.

"Good to see you, too, Fern. We're just on our way back to *Mamm* and *Dat*'s house. But driving up the road we saw you sitting there on the porch. I had to stop and see you, even though I reckon I'll see you later, since you're living right next door at the Weavers' house, now." He pulled her into a hug—brief but still a hug and an invitation into his well-guarded personal space.

She pulled back and looked him over again, wondering if the Amish dress was for their parents' benefit or his choice. "You've changed."

"Some." He nodded. "Not so terribly much, though. You still recognize me, at least." He must know what she meant, though. She wasn't talking about his appearance. He was different. Peaceful. He looked out over the rooftop. "I still have my quirks. I've just learned better how to live with them."

"I love your quirks, Martin, and I am so very happy to see you." She sensed Nick come up behind her. She supposed her parents had filled Martin in on her recent marriage, but she knew so little about what her brother was up to. "We have a lot to catch up on." She eyed the black car and his suspenders. "Have you joined the Beachy Amish?"

He gave her a blank look, then glanced down at his clothes and back at the car. "Oh. That. No." He shrugged.

Martin only ever answered the exact question, but she still knew how to read between his words. She guessed he was considering the option, but wouldn't say so. She wanted to ask more, but this wasn't the time to overwhelm him. Holding back the desire to know how long he was planning to stay, she leaned down to speak through the car window at her parents.

The smile on her *mamm*'s face proved how thrilled she was to have her boy back home, even if not for long. "Good to have you home again."

"Good to be home. I'm ready to sleep in my own bed." Her *dat* seemed in a good mood, as well. "We've got some news about Thomas and the farm to discuss, but I'd prefer to get unpacked first." He glanced back at his wife. "*Mamm* and I hoped you might come over later to talk?"

"And bring the *kinner*," her *mamm* added. "I miss them, and Martin can see how they've grown."

Fern was about to respond when the warmth of Nick's hand pressed lightly on the small of her back. He leaned close over her shoulder. The lightness of his palm against her back was a husband-like touch, and one he'd never shown her before. The sensation took her by surprise. Thankfully, he greeted her parents, taking their eyes off her.

Nick didn't seem to notice how affected she was, except for the almost imperceptible grin he was holding back. But to her family, he continued as though all was perfectly normal.

"You can all join us for supper tonight. The whole family will be there."

Her *mamm*'s eyes darted in Martin's direction, then back to Nick. "That's very nice of you, but we are tired from traveling. I think we'll have a quiet supper, but please do come over. If you can't get away this evening, then maybe tomorrow."

"We'll come, *Mamm*." At least Fern's voice sounded as though she'd collected her wits. She understood her mother's worries were for Martin in the big Weaver crowd, as much as her fatigue. "I'll bring you each a plate of food when we come."

"That will be nice. *Denki*, Fern." Her *mamm* leaned back against the seat, clearly relieved.

Beside them, the driver's side door shut as Martin got back in the car, so Fern and Nick stepped back. While her brother backed the car down the driveway, Nick draped one arm around her shoulders and waved with his other hand.

Again, the gesture seemed such a husband-like thing to do. He hadn't pretended before in front of her family—or anyone, for that matter. She wasn't sure what to make of it. From the way her stomach flipped around in a nervous fit, she was glad she'd barely eaten yet.

"We should get back home, too. I'm sure you're eager to talk to Martin." Nick's arm fell away and turned toward their abandoned lunch. "Did you get enough to eat?"

She nodded absently. Still processing her brother's arrival and Nick's unusual behavior, she took slow steps with food the last thing on her mind.

She wondered what news about Thomas and the farm could make her *dat*'s eyes light up rather than show the usual storm clouds that appeared at the mention of his former brother-in-law. Most of all, she wondered what was happening between her and Nick, and whether she could finally let down the guard she'd maintained for so many years to hold back her feelings for him.

"Kumm." Nick was waiting and motioned for her to join him. His good nature combined with a simple joy reflected in his eyes and the creases at their corners.

Fern stepped up beside him and dared to let herself feel what that might be like as they walked side by side. Being with Nick was more natural to her than being alone. No surprise, as they'd grown up practically beside one another. But this was more than palling around with a dear friend, and it felt as *wunderbar* as she'd always known it would.

Her heart continued to swell, like the hot-air balloons the town hosted on the Fourth of July as they filled before takeoff. And, if she wasn't mistaken, Nick had a lightness about him, as well. He stalled before they mounted the horses for the last part of the ride back to his parents' house. He didn't seem to want whatever this new thing between them was to end any more than she did.

"I think *Mamm* and *Dat* knew what they were doing," he said before offering her a lift back onto Sugar. He stayed close as she swung into the saddle, then rested his hand on the pommel, looking up at her. "I hope you've had as nice a day as I have."

"Ya." She couldn't have held back the wide smile spreading across her face if she'd tried. And she didn't even want to hide how happy she felt—not from herself or from Nick.

The corner of Nick's mouth tilted in satisfaction before he left her side, and soon they were making their way back. The yard was quiet as they rode up, and she supposed Eli had taken all the children on the hayride he promised.

Sure enough, while she and Nick brushed down the horses, the giggles and noise of a wagonload of young *kinner* rolled down the valley to the barn. Hurrying to greet them, she and Nick finished up their task and walked to the back field as the children jumped down from the hay wagon.

Their faces were bright red from the sun. Hay clung to their hair and clothes. And nary a one was concerned a bit. Beside her, Nick chuckled, then pulled her toward the small mob who were talking at the speed of lightning.

Fern caught sight of Cassie raising her arms to Josh so he could jump down safely, just at the same moment Josh's sight connected to hers.

"*Nay.* I want my *mamm. Kumm* and get me, *Mamm*," Josh hollered over the ruckus that suddenly went still. His little arms stretched out toward Fern, pleading for her to come.

How she adored that boy. If Fern's heart were a hot-air balloon, it was soaring above the clouds now. Cassie's arms fell to her side as she turned around with a smile for Fern. Just as quickly, Cassie's bright smile disappeared when her focus shifted to Nick.

The happy beat of Fern's heart stuttered. One glance at the pale, stricken expression on Nick's face was all it took to send the fragile flight of her joy crashing back down to earth.

Chapter Nine

Not yet.

That must be the answer to Nick's question about when he could move on. He was staring at his son, and Josh's pleas for his *mamm*—for Fern—rang in his ears. He'd sensed the joy in her deflate almost as rapidly as his own when she witnessed his reaction. And he hated that even worse than his own self-loathing for it.

She deserved Josh's love and affection, and his response stole the moment from her. He didn't want to, but grief came like this, in waves he couldn't control. He watched her quietly gather Josh into her arms and whisper something into his ear.

He tried to imagine what she said that caused his boy's lower lip to pucker until she kissed his little forehead, and all seemed well enough. Then he noticed Eli standing above it all, watching closely. His brother likely heard the exchange between Fern and Josh. Nick might ask him what she'd said.

Eli looked across at Nick and gave a slight shake of his head, telling him not to do something. What? Forbid his son from calling Fern *Mamm*? Chastise Fern? Nick wasn't sure what his brother thought he'd do. Nick hadn't figured that out himself, but he wouldn't do either of those things.

Yet, he couldn't help that the light of this day was draining from his soul. Just when he'd had hope—and joy—he'd failed so miserably to do the one thing he'd promised.

Josh would never think of Charity as his *mamm*. A fact that probably wasn't a surprise to anyone, but Nick was shocked by it all at once, no matter that his head had already known it.

He looked for Bethany and found her skipping along, flanked on either side by her cousins. If she'd noticed her brother calling Fern *Mamm*, she wasn't bothered by it. He was thankful his children were happy. And he knew Fern was the reason they were so well adjusted, which somehow made the dagger to his heart more painful.

Fern had seen his horror and shrank away from him the same as she'd done when he'd first seen her scar. He'd had no more control over that reaction than he'd had over the emotions that filled him this time. After all they'd put behind them earlier today, he'd made the same mistake all over again.

He turned from the scene and thought he could feel Fern watching him as he walked away. He intended to talk to her, try to undo the hurt he'd caused, but first he needed space to think. There was only one place he knew where he could be alone today. His store would be empty. He wouldn't do any work, but he'd find some peace—he hoped—before he bungled things even more.

The long walk to the store had worked out a good bit of Nick's stress, but the lonely silence in the building didn't bring the peace he'd hoped for. He'd walked back home in time for supper but didn't see Fern with the womenfolk finishing up the preparations. "Where's Fern?"

His *mamm* looked up from the breadbasket and dish of butter she'd placed on the table. "She took some food over to the Beilers. Said you'd seen them earlier and promised a plate. I'm sure she's happy to have them home."

"Ya." Nick glanced at Eli's wife, Sharon. He wasn't sure anyone knew Martin had come with the Beilers. He didn't want to be the one to let that slip, for sure. Eli's feelings regarding Martin were bound to be complicated. Deciding he had enough trouble of his own, he kept the news to himself. "We were supposed to go visit after supper."

His *mamm*'s eyebrows rose. "Fern said she'd just eat with her folks and not to wait for her."

Maybe she was avoiding him. After all, he'd been gone for hours, but did she expect him to come over to the Beilers or stay away? "Did she say when she'd be back?"

His *mamm* seemed to consider him closely before answering. "She's just next door. You could go ask her if it's an issue."

"Nay, I just wondered." He felt about as childish as his *mamm*'s gaze told him he was being. He'd eat his supper and go over as planned, although he wished he'd had a chance to explain himself to her first. He didn't relish the idea of his father-in-law witnessing the tension between them, but he wasn't going to stay away.

Not this time.

* * *

Fern arranged the food on her parents' table along with four place settings. Rhoda had been extra generous with the portions she sent over with Fern, even though she hadn't mentioned Martin was there. She thought it might be best to find out what her brother was up to before alerting everyone that he was home. Fern's *mamm* added a bowl of homemade applesauce and a jar of bread-and-butter pickles—Martin's favorite.

Once they were all seated, and their silent thanks given for the food, she finally relaxed. The commotion at the Weavers' had provided a great way for her upset to go unnoticed, but the quiet meal with her family soothed her frayed nerves.

Martin sat across from her and gave her an occasional questioning look, but it was her *dat* who spoke up.

"You look as tired as I feel. Is something bothering you?"

Unwilling to lie, she squirmed a bit with three sets of eyes on her now. "You mentioned something about Thomas Miller earlier…"

She let the sentence dangle, hoping to change the subject.

"Ah, that. Let's wait for Nick and tell the

tale only once." Her *dat* returned to eating his meal, satisfied there was nothing more on her mind. Her *mamm*'s gaze was the last to return to her food. Fern hadn't convinced her at all.

She also doubted Nick would come, not unless she went back to fetch him. And she wasn't about to drag an unwilling husband over to visit her parents. She wasn't quite ready to break the illusion Nick had given her family earlier that he was happy with her. Even if they all knew her marriage was a sham, she wasn't ready to have the obvious thrown in her face twice in one day.

She'd hurt Josh's feelings telling him to call her Fern, not *Mamm*, and her own heart broke in the process, too. She wasn't mad at Nick, not exactly. He couldn't help how he felt. She'd been shocked, too. But then he'd walked off and been gone the rest of the afternoon.

She swallowed some water to help the food past the lump in her throat, then looked at her brother. "How long will you be in town?"

"Just till tomorrow. I'll drive back on Saturday. The car isn't mine." So the car was a loaner from one of her uncle's Beachy friends or neighbors, and Martin didn't sound as though he regretted the excuse to keep his visit short.

Fern gave his suspenders a questioning glance. "Never got used to dressing *Englisch*." He shrugged and offered no more explanation.

The expression on her *mamm*'s face vacillated between disappointed and hopeful. "But he says he might come home more often...not stay away so long."

"Really? We'd all like that." She only wanted to encourage him, not pressure him. Martin wasn't shunned. He'd never made vows to the church. Whatever his reasons for staying away, he could come back anytime he wished. He just hadn't wanted to. He was private, and Fern knew to let him keep his reasons to himself.

"If you get word to me, I'll do my best to come and help the men raise your house." His offer was unforced and sincere. Martin had never been anything less than genuine and the gesture touched her.

"*Denki*, Martin." Fern jumped at the sound of Nick's voice. She hadn't heard him come into the house. He was standing in the doorway at the far end of the room and held a plate of cookies in one hand like a peace offering. He came to the table, put the cookies down, then rested his hands on the back of the empty chair next to Fern.

"May I?" He needn't ask, but his blue eyes held hers as if she could deny him.

She nodded.

As he sat down beside her, she kept her focus on the table rather than the quizzing glances she was sure passed between her parents. Since when did a husband ask to sit by his wife? Or since when did Nick ever have to ask to sit at their table? He'd always been welcome in the Beilers' home whenever—and to sit wher-ever—he wanted. Still, he had asked her per-mission this time and with more apology than she thought she'd ever heard in his voice.

He slid his chair closer to hers, leaving a very narrow space between them and leaning close to her ear. *"Denki."*

He truly made staying mad difficult. But forgiving him didn't erase the pain she'd seen on his face earlier. Or the near impossibility it wouldn't happen again. His promise to Charity would always be between them now.

Her *mamm* cut through the awkward silence, saving Fern from making a response.

"Shall we make some *kaffi* to go with the cookies?" Her *mamm* was gathering up the empty plates and directed her question at Fern. "How about you get it started while I grab these dishes?"

Fern stood, and Nick did, as well. He reached for an empty serving bowl to help clear the table, but her *mamm* swatted his hand away. "That's unnecessary, Nick. You stay here with the menfolk. We'll only be a minute."

Nick shot a pleading look at Fern, as if she might intervene. She wasn't sure why Nick would be desperate to help with the dishes. And just as she realized he wanted a chance to speak privately, her *mamm* hurried her off as though the cookies might rise up on legs and disappear before the coffee could percolate.

As soon as her mother was out of sight in the kitchen, Fern's *dat* snitched a cookie from the plate. He waggled his eyebrows at Fern and took a bite.

Fern giggled as she walked into the kitchen. Maybe *Mamm* was right.

"Your *dat* took a cookie, didn't he?" The half-hidden smile on her *mamm*'s face removed any genuine anger from her scolding tone and the teasing shake of her finger. "That man."

Her parents' good humor implied the trip had been a pleasant one. Fern hoped her grandmother was finding her new home pleasant, too. "How was *Grossmammi* when you left her?"

"She's adjusting. Or I suppose, the rest of

the family is adjusting to her." There was no criticism in the statement, although Fern could imagine the transition might take some getting used to for everyone. "The biggest surprise of it all was Martin. Of course, your *grossmammi* is a mastermind at getting her way. Once she made up her mind to find a way to get Martin to come back to Promise ... Well, Martin didn't stand a chance of hiding from her. When he hadn't come around for almost a week, she followed him right on out to his honey house where he'd been spending all his time taking care of those bees of his."

Rather than disapproval, her *mamm*'s voice was bursting with gratitude. After years of worry over Martin since he'd left, her *mamm*'s relief was palpable. "That's why I wanted to talk to you before we get sidetracked with all this about Thomas and the farm. Martin's not happy in the *Englisch* world. He hasn't said so, but I think he might consider coming home— with the right motivation. He's considering joining the Beachy Amish... That would be all right..."

"But you'd rather have him close." Fern understood the feeling completely, but there was a hint in her *mamm*'s tone that she wanted to bring Fern into her confidence. She was up to something. Maybe *Grossmammi* had rubbed off on her *mamm* a bit.

"You know, Martin always keeps his word. If he says a thing, he means it. And his offer to help build your house… It's hopeful, ain't so?" Her *mamm*'s fingers fidgeted with her apron. "Make sure you find a way to stay in touch. He'll come if you ask him."

Fern placed a hand on her *mamm*'s shoulder. "Don't fret so. Of course I'll invite him to come. I'll make sure of it."

"*Denki*, Fern. I know you will." Her *mamm* let out a slow breath. "Now, you go on back in there. You know your *dat*. More than likely, he won't wait any longer to tell the news about Thomas than he can wait for dessert."

Fern stalled. She was curious about Thomas, but loath to add any more upset to a day that had felt like a roller-coaster ride of emotions. She'd rather ease along a while before another big rise and fall, but there was nothing for it. She'd have to face whatever her *dat* so urgently wanted to share.

Her *mamm* gathered five coffee mugs together onto a tray with cream and sugar and passed it to Fern. "Take these to the table." *Mamm* shooed her out of the kitchen. "I'll bring the *kaffi* soon as it's ready."

* * *

Nick stalled the conversation about Thomas as best he could until Fern finally came back. Ezekiel was about to burst, waiting to tell him whatever he'd discovered while they were gone. Nick figured it was similar to the rumor Cassie had shared—and he hadn't remembered to tell Fern yet. He sure didn't want to have to tell her he'd heard it not once, but twice, before she knew anything about it. Maybe she wouldn't care.

Nay, he knew better than that. Besides, he had no desire to be the kind of husband who left his wife out of important discussions. If for no other reason than because he wouldn't appreciate if she treated him that way. The Lord wanted his followers to treat others as they wished to be treated themselves. He'd heard that sermon enough times never to forget it.

"Finally," Ezekiel stated good-naturedly as Fern returned from the kitchen. "Now about this business with Thomas Miller."

Fern settled into the seat next to him. Where Nick had adjusted his chair a little nearer to hers when he sat down, she now moved hers enough to keep from brushing up against him.

Nick held back a sigh. He had a lot of repairs to make for running off today.

Ezekiel cleared his throat. "I learned some interesting facts down at my brother's place." He paused, making sure he had their attention. "The Realtor Thomas is using—was using—his wife's cousin isn't Amish, but he does a lot of business with Amish. Keeping them happy is in his own best interest. When rumors from up here in Promise started circulating down in the valley, he pulled the plug on his deal with Thomas for your land."

"Ada's land, you mean."

"*Nay*, my *mamm* always intended that land for Charity, then for you and the *kinner*, and in the end, for Fern. She doesn't feel like he stole the land from her, but from you. Both of you. Now, we may follow the Lord's command and turn the other cheek at this wrong done to us, but the Lord is just. Perhaps it is because of this justice that Thomas can no longer sell the land for such a high price. Without the interest of big-developer money, he'll have to settle for a fair price— something a farmer could pay. And that gives us a chance to keep the land among the Amish."

So Cassie had the story straight. If Ezekiel was wondering what to tell other Amish who may be interesting in buying the farm, the fact that Nick was still out of the running hadn't changed.

Nick glanced at Fern. She wrapped a napkin around her finger and twisted it back and forth. Whatever she was thinking, she was concentrating deeply. He wished they'd discussed this together, so he'd have some idea what was going through her mind.

He stuck with a safe reply. "It would be *better* for the land to stay Amish, if possible. There's so little useful and affordable farmland these days. I'd hate to see us lose this."

"So, you may want to reconsider your decision to build on your store, and buy the farm yourself after all."

Out of the corner of his eye, Nick saw Fern's head swing fully around to face him directly. He met her gaze but was at a loss to decipher which emotion lay behind those dark eyes.

Together, they were about to build a home—designed to suit Fern. Because more than anything, Nick wanted Fern to have a home that she could make her own and where they could make new memories. If today had taught him anything, it was that he couldn't stay stuck in the past. He didn't know how or if he could keep his promise to Charity, but he'd do his best to keep the ones he'd made to Fern.

"*Nay*, what's done is done, for better or for worse." His words came too hastily, perhaps.

He still had no assurance that he could manage this precarious balance between his past promises and the future his renewed feelings for Fern made him hope for. But somehow, beneath all his doubts, he sensed the rightness of this decision. "Let the others know I won't be making an offer. If the farm is going to pass to Amish hands, they won't be mine."

Beside him, Fern drew in a sudden gasp of breath. The confusion on her face made him instantly aware he ought to have discussed it with her first. The surety he'd felt moments ago wavered. Had he misjudged? He'd believed the decision would please her. "Don't you want to think about it, Nick?"

He was tired of thinking and wanted to move forward with his life—*their* life. Not that Charity's memory would disappear, but fresh memories had to be made, too. He rubbed at the tight knot forming at the back of his neck.

"*Kaffi*'s ready." Leah, with coffeepot in hand, entered with a smile broad enough to infer she had the cure for all their problems in that single brew.

Would that she did.

As her *mamm* dispensed steaming hot coffee into everyone's mugs, Fern turned and leaned forward, so that only Nick could hear her. "Have you forgotten about my savings? If the price has gone down enough…" Fern paused as Leah leaned over to fill Nick's mug.

Nick shook his head. Why would she want to change their plans, unless he'd completely misjudged what was happening between them? Her hand came to rest on his knee. "Can't we talk about it?"

There was no sense in denying such a reasonable request. He ought to have discussed it with her before responding in the first place, but he'd not expected her to want to buy the farm. While he'd grieved the loss of the farm after their move to his parents' house, Fern had only changed for the better. He believed she was happier because, once away from the farm, she had the chance to grow into her role as a member of his family and as his wife rather than the children's caregiver in another woman's house. The awkwardness between them had disappeared, which brought him a great deal of comfort.

Had he misjudged so badly?

"Think about it for a few days, *ya?*" There was no real question in Ezekiel's statement. He was offering a way out of the apparent mistake Nick had just made and saving Fern and Nick both any embarrassment.

Gott sure had blessed him in the father-in-law department this time.

Grateful, Nick nodded.

Fern leaned back in her chair and glanced upward as she did when she was silently thanking the Almighty for something.

Now that Nick had an idea of what it could be like to love Fern and be loved back, his desire to make a new home with her had only grown. In his mind, returning to the farm would be a setback. For sure and certain he needed more divine help than ever to get Fern to agree with him.

Chapter Ten

The days were getting longer and sunlight lasting well beyond the supper hour. And every minute of the past couple of days since their Ascension Day fun had been busy, making the days longer still.

Across from her at the supper table, Josh's head drooped with sleepiness until his sweet face barely missed a head-on landing in his mashed potatoes. Muffled laughter spilled over from the rest of the family around the table.

"Poor *boppli*," she said, catching Nick's gaze and noting the amusement on his face. "I ought to take him on up to bed." Fern was about as tired as Josh herself.

Nick's chair squeaked against the wood floor as he pushed back from the table. "I'll carry him."

Josh's head lolled to one side as Nick lifted

him from beneath his little arms. Fern grabbed a napkin and leaned forward to give a hurried swipe at the food all over his rosy face before Nick gently turned his son around to rest against his chest.

Following behind Nick to the *kinner*'s bedroom, Fern tried not to think overmuch about how the sight of father and son filled her heart to overflowing. Her feelings for Nick were growing harder to contain. Yet the moment was one to cherish. The kind to be recalled when life was hard or tiring. Or when someone you loved so dear was gone, either by a long distance or to heaven.

Martin had left again today and memories of growing up were all she had to keep him close. *Ya*, the heart-filling moments like this weren't meant to be buried but held tight.

She just didn't know how she was supposed to manage so much love and not end up stitching the severed pieces of her heart together like a patchwork quilt when it swelled too large for the kind of marriage she'd agreed to.

Standing beside the bed, Nick rounded to face her. In a low tone over the top of Josh's rumpled hair, he asked, "Can you undo his suspenders? We'll let him just sleep in his clothes tonight, rather than wake him to undress."

With care, Fern began to remove his suspenders. As her hand passed across Nick's chest to reach the front side and release the snaps, the heat of Nick's gaze stilled her. She swallowed at the way her heart leaped up into her throat and rushed to complete the task.

"Tickles, *Mamm*. Tickles me." Josh squirmed. His eyes opened, then weighed back down with sleep.

Fern froze, not daring to look up and see Nick's eyes again. Her face heated and her fingers fidgeted with her prayer *kapp* as she stepped aside, keeping her head down and pulling the bedsheets back.

After what seemed an age, Nick sighed before bending low to lay Josh on the bed and tuck the covers around him. Fern lowered herself to place a soft kiss on the precious cheek still upturned as the other side of his face nestled into his pillow.

"Night, *Mamm*," he mumbled so quietly Fern hoped Nick couldn't hear.

With a hand over her heart to keep it from thumping out of her chest, Fern shuffled to flee the room, but Nick's fingers caught her elbow.

"*Bitte*, Fern." His whispered plea matched the tension emanating from him as he came close behind her. "Please *kumm* outside and speak with me. Don't hide from me."

Nick reached for her hand. His hold was tentative, offering the chance to pull away. She couldn't. Didn't. Even if refusing his hand was the wise thing to do, she couldn't will herself to refuse the tenderness of his touch, and his fingers entwined in hers.

"A walk?" Nick asked.

The fatigue weighing her down at supper lessened. They hadn't had much of a chance to talk since her *dat* revealed Thomas's farm was going to be sold at a better price. Friday and Saturday were always busy at the store, but even more so after being closed on Thursday this week. And Fern had spent as much time as possible with Martin before he left.

"A walk would be nice," she agreed.

Keeping her hand in his, Nick led her down the hall, pausing only to grab a flashlight from his room. On the way past the kitchen, he let his parents know they'd be gone a while, then they headed out the door of the farmhouse with no more explanation.

The behavior was a far cry from the grieving soul Nick had been for the past two years. Tonight, as they strolled beyond the house toward the fields with the sun just dipping below the mountain peaks on the horizon, this was more like the adventurous and playful Nick of old, yet she couldn't exactly pin this as one of their childhood larks.

Nay, there was so much more behind these feelings than any she'd experienced before. Was she imagining it?

She sighed. Why was it so instinctual to explain away anything that felt like Nick may have growing feelings for her? If she'd been so mistaken about his feelings for her after the fire, she must have been doing this even then.

Trying her best not to erect a wall around her heart, Fern forced her mind not to pass off what was happening as anything less meaningful than exactly how it appeared.

Still, the look of grief he'd shown when Josh called her *Mamm* warned her to be cautious.

"Should we keep going to the gate or jump the fence here?" Nick came to a stop by the old chestnut fence between the Weaver property boundary and a rutted dirt road that led to an old hunting cabin much farther off the beaten path.

"If we're headed to the cabin, it makes more sense to cross here." The fence wasn't high or difficult to climb. Although she couldn't bound over it in a single giant leap the way Nick did.

He held his hand out to help her over. She hesitated. The fading daylight cast dark shadows along the ground. "Can you shine the light so I can see where to place my foot?"

Fern rested one hand on the top plank of the fence, watching for the light to guide her first step. But instead of using the flashlight to aid her, Nick placed a powerful arm under her outstretched one and around her back, then with his other arm he swept around the back of her legs and lifted her feet off the ground.

Instinctively, she wrapped her arms around Nick's neck to remain balanced as he swung her over the fence and pulled her to him. As the motion stilled and her swimming head sorted what had just happened, she loosened her grip on him. Only he didn't set her down right away. Still cradling her in his arms and breathless, he looked down at her.

"I know how he feels." His blue eyes roamed her face while she puzzled over whom he was talking about. "Josh, I mean. I know how it is to think of you first thing on waking or want to run to you when you come into a room." He gently lowered her legs to the ground, but kept her close to him. "And for you to be the last one on my mind as I go to sleep."

Fern's heart stuttered, and she thought her

legs might give way. He'd put her down too soon, if he was going to say things like that to her. "You do?"

His hands slipped up to rest on each of her shoulders. "I won't stop him from calling you *Mamm*. If *Gott* has seen fit for you to be the only mother he really knows, who am I to question it?"

Fern wasn't sure what he meant exactly. The words were well meant, she could tell. He felt them deeply. But he hadn't said that *he* would choose her to be a *mamm* for Josh. He'd simply acknowledged the fact that *Gott* had.

"*Ya. Gott* has made it so." Why wasn't that enough? She stepped away, far enough to cause his arms to fall back to his sides. Perhaps she shouldn't want more. But *ach*, her heart yearned to be Nick's choice—not his only option.

What had he said wrong?

Nick was still puzzling out where he'd made his mistake last night as he dressed the next morning. He couldn't figure if Fern was just too stubborn to acknowledge his feelings for her or if he was truly so bad at expressing them.

He'd embarked on that walk hoping to explain his desire to let the opportunity to buy the farm go to someone else. What he wanted was a fair shot at making a home of their own—his and Fern's. He still did. But the sadness in her voice as she stated her role in his life was because *Gott* had made it so caught him off guard, caused him to question whether Fern shared in his desire at all.

Then she'd pulled away and the moment he'd hoped for had been cast to the wind.

He hadn't been able to clear up anything between them, and his frustration only led to another restless night. At least today was the Lord's Day and a Visiting Sunday, too. He wouldn't have to worry about falling asleep in church or being too muddle-headed to get his work done at the store.

After breakfast, his *dat* read the Bible passage chosen for this week's lesson, as all the members of the church would do at home today. They sang two songs, one traditional and the other a children's favorite, before they left the table to enjoy a quiet morning at home.

Most visiting took place after lunch, but the Beilers had invited them all next door to eat together. So, Fern slipped away to go help her *mamm*, and Nick followed her out to the porch.

The weather was pleasant this time of year before summer's humidity settled in. The wind chimes jingled in a warm southerly breeze right before the rumble of a vehicle turned into the Beilers' drive.

Fern stopped at the base of the porch steps and looked up over her shoulder at him. "Who could that be?"

Curious, Nick cleared two steps at a time to join her at the bottom and go see. Halfway across the distance between the two houses, the van door opened, and Ada stepped out.

"Grossmammi?" Fern's brows pinched together as she turned to Nick. "On a Sunday... and right after *Mamm* and *Dat* just got back. It doesn't make sense. What is she doing here?"

Nick almost laughed. As if he ever knew what Ada Beiler was up to, but this had to be too serious of a matter to joke about. "I'm sure we are about to find out."

He watched Fern's expression change, growing more concerned with each second.

"Don't." He laid his hand on her arm. "Don't imagine every bad thing that could have happened. I'm sure there's an explanation and everything will work out."

Her eyes darted away, and she bit the inside of her lip, then sighed. "You always say that. How can you know everything will be all right?"

"I don't know how it will work out. I just

know how easy it is to assume the worst and most times the worst never happens."

"Sometimes it does."

"*Ya*, sometimes. And then we make it through." He and Fern always did.

The lines on her forehead melted and the deep brown in her eyes brightened. "We do, don't we?"

It took every muscle in his body to hold back the urge to hold her face in his hands and kiss her. How could she not know? "We're a team, you and I. We always have been."

She squeezed his fingers and nodded. The contact was sweet, brief and had to be enough. For now.

Somehow, he'd knock down that infernal wall she'd built to keep her heart from him. Because his heart was filling up with more than friendly care for her, and he was coming to understand that it had been for quite some time.

Fern walked her grandmother into the house while Nick retrieved her bags from the back of the van. Holding the door open, she looked over her shoulder to see if Nick was coming. Rather than just behind them as Fern expected, Nick was still at the van and half-hidden by a growing stack of boxes.

When he saw she was waiting, he raised his hands out beside his shoulders and gave a what-in-the-world shrug. Fern pivoted her attention to her grandmother passing through the open door as Fern held it, stunned.

Grossmammi smiled sweetly up at Fern as though nothing unusual was happening, even though Nick and the driver were still outside unloading boxes. Fern wasn't sure she had taken this many things with her when she moved to live with Titus in the first place.

"Grossmammi?" Fern stepped into the house behind her. "What is going on?"

Her *dat*'s voice echoed her question. Dressed in his Sunday best, without his jacket on, he stood up from his favorite chair on the far side of the family room. Her *mamm* appeared in the open space between them and the kitchen. She held her hands, coated in floury biscuit dough, together in front of her as she surveyed the room.

Color drained from her *mamm*'s face. "What is it? Nothing bad…"

Grossmammi, looking rather pleased considering all the upheaval she was causing, said, *"Nay,* nothing is the matter. Thomas decided to give the cottage back to me. He was in a mighty big hurry to do so before the elders could call a special meeting to discuss the matter. And I came back before that wife of his could change his mind, like she's done so often."

Grossmammi plopped down on the sofa. She sure seemed spryer than when she'd left just a couple of months ago. She wasn't shuffling like she did in the cold weather...which had been one of her supposed reasons for moving down to the valley.

"That is *wunderbar gut* news." The relief in her *dat*'s voice was mirrored in the way her *mamm*'s shoulders also relaxed. "Though it's curious that you came on a Sunday. Why not wait another day or two?"

She opened her mouth to answer when a loud thumping at the front door distracted them all. Nick stumbled through the doorway with an armload four boxes high.

Fern jumped up to help. She removed the top crate, revealing the tip of his hat. He leaned backward, adjusting the load.

"*Denki*...whoever you are." He laughed before peeking around the boxes to see Fern. In a low voice, he added, "The driver has been very informative. I'll tell you what he said when we finish unloading."

Her *dat* came to help stack the boxes as Nick

hauled them inside. Fern's *mamm* had washed her hands and sat with *Grossmammi* on the couch, so Fern took the love seat, which left two chairs for her *dat* and Nick.

But Nick squeezed in beside her on the love seat instead. Whoever designed this two-seater must have measured for one and a half. Only two children would fit comfortably. Nick tilted his shoulders, reached behind her and rested his arm along the back of the seat, perhaps to make more room. It didn't help. The heat of a blush warmed her cheeks. If anything, it was more intimate, even though everyone pretended not to notice.

Except for *Grossmammi*, who appeared supremely delighted.

Soon all eyes were fixed on her grandmother anyway, waiting for the answer to the reason for her hurry. "It may be Sunday, but my ox is in the ditch." Eyebrows rose at her reference to the biblical analogy about the Sabbath being for man, not man for the Sabbath. "I couldn't wait. Thomas is coming tomorrow. And that can only mean trouble." *Grossmammi*'s gaze came to rest on Fern and Nick. "For you."

"Not if we don't let it." Nick shook his head. "The farm is none of my business anymore. What harm can Thomas do?"

"He has his ways." Fern's *dat* murmured.

Fern's *mamm* was slow to speak, but now she entered the conversation in her soft-spoken manner. "Let's not borrow trouble. Tomorrow will bring what it will, and the Lord *Gott* will give us the strength and wisdom to bear it, if we ask. I have prayed for a change of heart in Thomas. And who would have thought Ada would return to her cottage? We cannot know what *Gott* is doing in a man's heart."

Her *mamm*'s face reddened. She didn't often speak up. Fern's own face warmed, but with a touch of shame, as did the others.

Her *dat* cleared his throat. "You are right, Leah, as always. We must remain in prayer over this matter in our hearts today."

Nick's hand came to rest on Fern's shoulder with a comforting squeeze.

More and more she was hard-pressed to ignore how having Nick beside her in these moments was only a convenient arrangement between two friends. He'd always been protective, but this was different—and amazingly close to how she'd always imagined it might feel to be cherished, as a man's wife.

She longed to lean into the invitation of his care. All night long, she'd regretted moving away from him so hastily after he'd expressed his wish for Josh to call her *Mamm*. Once again, she'd allowed her old insecurities to haunt a special moment.

But one thing was for sure and certain, she didn't feel like *Poor Fern* sitting here, almost in Nick's arms. All she'd have to do is relax—just an inch.

Just as quick, her chance slipped away. The moment was lost as her *mamm* excused herself to go prepare lunch, and her *dat* strode across the room to inspect the pile of boxes lining the wall of the entryway.

"Fern, are you okay?" Nick's finger brushed the edge of her scar, sending a tingle down her spine as he pulled his hand back. "Don't worry about Thomas."

Thomas? She hadn't been thinking of him. *Nay*, she'd forgotten about it all for one blissful minute—a lapse of memory she couldn't let happen again.

She gave him a weak smile and got up to go help her *mamm*, wishing the foreboding feeling in the pit of her stomach would go away. And she couldn't help but notice that Nick hadn't promised it would all work out this time.

Chapter Eleven

The following day, Nick found concentrating on his work at the store difficult. Fern was helping Ada move back into her cottage. But she was also determined to go over to the farm and dig up the potato patch she'd planted back in early March. The crop wouldn't be full grown yet, but she expected a nice bushel of small, new potatoes. Nick chuckled. There was no way she was letting those potatoes go to waste.

If Thomas arrived in Promise today, he'd likely go straight to the farm, and Nick didn't like the idea of Fern left alone there with him.

Of course, he hadn't said so. He'd sound ridiculously suspicious. Thomas never posed a physical threat of any kind to anyone, but Charity had always left his presence shaken.

A person's words could sting, even if his hands never did.

As Leah and Ezekiel Beiler wisely recommended yesterday, Nick had prayed a great deal over the past twenty-four hours. The result was an urgent need to settle a date for the construction of the addition to the store. He couldn't wait any longer. The time had come to break his family away from this drama. He couldn't help but believe this new home of theirs would bring them peace—and healing.

The melancholy that wrapped around Fern with the mention of Thomas proved Nick's instinct to let the farm go had been right. There was some connection causing her to pull away from him, the same as she'd done after the accident, and he had to do whatever it took to break it.

The wall clock noted the time as ten to one. He walked behind the counter and around the corner to the deli to see if Cassie was back from her lunch break. Susie Yoder, one of his part-time workers, was behind the deli counter slicing meat for a customer.

"Is Cassie back yet?"

Susie looked up from her task. "She was in the back when I put the sandwiches you asked for in there."

"Denki." Nick pushed through the staff access door to the bakery behind the deli. Sure enough, Cassie was slicing and bagging the fresh bread she'd baked that morning. She looked up at his approach. "Did you see your *dat* at home?"

"Ya, I gave him your message. He said he'd talk to the bishop right away. He believes they can make quick arrangements for the barn raising—or house raising—soon. Everyone is already expecting it."

What a relief. At least one worry was getting taken care of, thank the Lord. "And your *bruder*?"

"Zach said he'd be here early, by two." Taking off a pair of disposable gloves for handling the food, Cassie surveyed the tidy stacks of bagged bread loaves on the work cart. "That ought to be enough for this afternoon, don't you think?"

Nick nodded, thankful also for the nearness of his family and all the ways they helped him. "I'll transfer them out to the sales racks.

"Denki, Cassie." As he backed out the door, this time pulling the loaded cart with him, she smiled back with understanding that his gratitude was for more than the bread.

Once Zach arrived to take care of customers at the checkout, Nick headed up the lane to check on Fern at the farm. Of course, there was a good possibility he'd also run into Thomas. He steeled himself for the encounter, knowing it made sense to get this conversation over and done. Once he let Thomas know he still wasn't interested in buying the property, all his business with Thomas would be finished, other than normal exchanges of pleasantries when their paths crossed. And since Thomas rarely acted in a grandfatherly way for Bethany or Josh, that wouldn't be often.

The afternoon sun shone in his eyes, causing him to squint. The temperatures peaked about this time of day, and he began to sweat hiking uphill to the farm. But the hope he was finally going to get closure and some of these weighty matters settled pumped extra blood through his veins and invigorated him.

As he neared Ada's cottage, he saw Fern by the greenhouse, washing potatoes under the outdoor spigot.

"I see you got that chore done," he called to her while cutting across the yard to meet her. Nearer, he noticed her bare feet and muddy apron from digging.

She straightened and raised a wrist to her forehead to look in his direction. Her face was pink, either from the heat, too much sun or both. Strange how the view of her made his heart jump up to his throat.

"You're a sight for sore eyes." He cringed inwardly at the terrible attempt at a compliment. But she did present a pretty picture standing there with rosy cheeks, the mountain behind her and the sunlight reflecting gold in her hair.

Either she didn't hear him, or she chose to ignore his statement.

He held up the brown bag in his hand. "Have you eaten lunch yet? I brought sandwiches and the salt-and-vinegar chips you like."

"The chips sound *wunderbar.* I ate a little something with *Grossmammi* earlier, but I am hungry again." She glanced at her dirty apron and hands. "I'll be right back. On the porch?"

He nodded and walked to the front of the cottage, while Fern slipped in the back door. A breeze swept across Ada's front porch and cooled him as he rocked on the swing. After a few minutes, Fern joined him wearing a clean apron and carrying two glasses of lemonade. She placed the drinks on the small table between the porch swing and the chair where she sat.

If she was distressed, he saw no sign of it. Apparently, he'd been worried all morning for no reason. Borrowing trouble, like Leah had said. Relieved, he bowed his head for their silent thanks for the food before they began to eat.

"Ach." Fern covered her mouth with her fingers and finished the bite in her mouth before continuing. "Thomas spoke to me earlier, on his way to the house. He said he'd like to talk to you, but not at the store. He asked if you'd come see him when it suited you today." She lifted the glass to her lips and took a swallow. "He was pleasant, actually."

"Was he?" Suspicion laced his response. Not that Nick didn't believe her.

"Ya. What do you suppose that means?" Her eyebrow rose.

"No idea. Maybe your *mamm*'s prayers are working." He shrugged.

"Perhaps. *Mamm* always seems to have more faith than the rest of us. For certain sure, when she prays, she believes with all her heart *Gott* can do anything."

Nick was glad someone had faith to pray the way Leah did because he'd given up hope years ago that Thomas would ever change. "I reckon I may as well head over there when I finish eating."

"Ya, get it over with." Fern reached across the space between them and laid her hand on

his. He was aware she'd done so with no fore-thought and definitely unaware of how the touch made his pulse race. "Do you want me to go with you?"

"As nice as that would be, there's no need. You've plenty else to do."

And as much as he'd like to believe Thomas had some significant change of heart and mo-tive, Nick would be very surprised if this chat was a pleasant one. More likely, he was furious about pressure from the church to give Ada the cottage. He might have hidden his anger from Fern for a few minutes, but no doubt the truth would come out.

And the last thing Nick wanted to do was subject Fern to the other side of Thomas Miller. Chasing the rest of his sandwich down with lemonade, he stood. "Sorry to rush off, Fern, but I need to get back to the store. And what I have to say to Thomas won't take long."

"So you've decided about the house, then?" Fern stood, too. "We haven't talked about it since *Dat* first told us it was back on the mar-ket. Have you considered using my savings… our savings?"

"I meant to talk about it. I guess there never seemed to be the right time. I know that's not much of an excuse." He rubbed at the back of his neck. Marriage didn't work too well if you didn't talk about the important things. He knew that. "I don't know how to explain this, but my heart is telling me to let the farm go. I've prayed and thought about it, almost constantly, and the feeling doesn't go away. I even asked Eli to set a date for raising our house." Another thing he should have discussed with her. He winced. "I'm sorry I didn't talk to you about that, either."

"I'm not angry, Nick." She brushed at some crumbs clinging to her skirt, as if stalling. "But why? Losing the farm was so painful for you. And all you wanted these past two years was to keep everything the same. And now, we have a chance to do that."

"*Ya*, it was painful... But maybe it was necessary, Fern. I was doing my best to keep my promise to Charity, but..." But *Gott* had other plans, which seemed blatantly obvious after all that had happened. Only Nick had no business claiming to know the mind of *Gott*. "I wonder if *Gott* is trying to show me—us—a different way."

Fern leaned against the wall behind her for support. Myriad emotions displayed on her face.

"Maybe I should put off going to speak with Thomas, so we can talk about this more later."

Fern shook her head in disagreement.

"There's no need to wait. Not if you must do this to find peace in your heart. I understand."

"I want to do this for you, Fern, for you to have peace…for all of us to move forward as a family." Getting those feelings out in the open felt better than he expected, like a load lifted from his back.

But Fern didn't react so well. She groped for the arm of the rocking chair and then sat down again. "Fern, you're pale. Can I get you something?" He picked up their empty glasses. "Some water?"

She rested a moment and slowly her color returned. "I'm fine. Maybe just a little too much sun."

He wasn't so sure. "Maybe I should get you a drink, anyway."

"*Nay.* You go on. What you said… It just surprised me, is all." She took the glass from him, then glanced up, so that their eyes met for several heartbeats before she spoke. "A *happy* surprise." She smiled, easing his concern. "I enjoyed spending this time with you, Nick. It was unexpected, but nice, for sure."

Now, that was promising. A smile of his own eased across his face. "Me, too. Being with you, I mean, and talking about things. It was *gut*, for sure."

Wishing he could linger there with her, he said goodbye instead and turned to go, more determined than ever to set his plans for their future in motion. And that began with putting Thomas Miller squarely in his past.

Not thirty minutes after he'd left her, Fern caught sight of Nick walking briskly back down the lane. She was carrying laundry from the clothesline, where the warm day and steady breeze quickly dried the children's clothes she'd brought with her to wash while helping her grandmother settle back in at the cottage.

Nick waved as he passed, and Fern shifted the basket to one hip to wave back.

I want to do this for you... She'd heard him with her own ears or else she wouldn't believe he'd go so far as to let the farm go for her sake—to move forward as a family. The revelation made her a little weak in the knees. It was so unexpected. Her *mamm* was praying for Thomas to have a change of heart, but maybe Nick was the one whose heart was changing.

Did she dare hope?

Ach, but she couldn't spend the rest of the afternoon woolgathering. Her grandmother's return was one extra bit of work on top of an already busy week for the Weaver family, since

Nick's brother was hosting church this coming Sunday. That meant even extended family would pitch in to help Eli and his wife, Sharon, to get ready for both the service and the meal which followed for the whole congregation. Fern and Rhoda would both be working double time to help with all the cooking and cleaning to be done. And Rhoda was doing most of the week's laundry alone, while Fern helped her grandmother.

At least her *mamm* had taken Josh to help them out while Bethany was at school, but Fern should go get him soon. Hurrying in the back door with the laundry, she began folding the clothes to take back with her. The ironing would have to wait.

A loud knock came from the front of the house. Quickly, she picked up the last pair of Josh's pants to fold, and the knocking increased.

"Grossmammi?"

No answer. She was likely taking a nap, and nothing roused her until she was ready.

"Coming," Fern called. Whoever was at the door certainly didn't possess much patience, so she oughtn't have been so surprised when she opened it to Thomas Miller looking rather like a summer storm cloud.

She took a deep breath. "Thomas, how can I help you?"

"Fern." His demeanor changed as quickly as the threat of rain could suddenly pass in the opposite direction this time of year. "I was hoping to speak with Ada."

Suddenly feeling protective of her grandmother, Fern stepped outside, leaving Thomas no choice but to step aside.

She closed the screen door behind her. "*Grossmammi*'s exhausted from her trip and resting."

"*Ya*, well, let her know I stopped by." Thomas paused, ran his fingers through his long beard, then looked at her for an uncomfortable few seconds. "I had an enlightening conversation with your husband." His lips puckered when he said *your husband* as though he'd swallowed a bug. "Interesting, don't you think, that he would turn down such an extraordinarily generous price? I practically offered to give him the farm."

Rather unbelievable, she thought, that Thomas would practically give away anything. But it was the subtle disrespect for Nick in his tone that gave her the greatest concern and put her on the defensive. "He has his reasons."

"Oh, believe me, I understand perfectly. Nick and I have a lot in common, you know."

"*Nay*, I can't say I know any such a thing." Nick was nothing like Thomas. Fern wished she was still behind the door. She'd like to slam it and be done with this horrible conversation. God forgive her.

Thomas stepped lazily toward the steps, then leaned against the post and continued to explain. "Becoming a widower at a young age is a trial, for sure. I always knew that someday Nick would come to understand my side of things. Folks around here, no offense to you, have been almost self-righteous in their judgment of me, as if I had no right to move on with my life."

Fern stepped back. One more word from him and she was afraid of what she might say. He was insulting everyone she loved. The Beilers and the Weavers had both suffered because of his choices, and never once sought retribution against him. Whatever opinions others had of him were of his own making.

"No offense, Fern, dear. I don't mean you." He stepped forward, erasing the space she'd just put between them. "You must be delighted now that Nick has come to the same conclusion as I was forced to all those years ago. I could see there was no use arguing with your husband on the issue. He's determined to sacrifice his happiness for yours, as any decent husband ought to do."

Never in her life had turning the other cheek been as hard as it was in this moment. The insinuation that Nick's actions resembled the way Thomas abandoned Charity was hateful and untrue. Yet, he smiled at her as if he held a secret known just between them. She fairly shook from holding back the angry words on her tongue.

"I reckon you've said enough." *Grossmammi*'s voice startled them both before she stepped out onto the porch.

Thomas smiled as innocently as he'd done throughout his entire speech. Nothing more than a slight twitch in his right hand gave away the effect her grandmother had on him. "I was just leaving." He backed away, giving Fern room to breathe again. "Your granddaughter says you are tired, so I'll come back at a better time."

He left without once looking directly at *Grossmammi*.

"A snake in the grass, that one. Don't you pay any heed to a word he says." She just about jerked the screen door from its hinges as she opened it for them to return inside. "I think I'd better lie back down. *Denki*, for all you did to help me today, *Liebling*. Now, you go on back to your family. They'll be needing you, too."

Fern wished she could so easily disregard the accusations Thomas made about Nick. But there was a bit of truth in them that nagged at her thoughts. Nick was sacrificing an awful lot for her sake. Just before Thomas had arrived, that very knowledge had warmed her heart and given her hope. Nick's declaration had touched her deeply, almost completely overwhelmed her. But in reality, Nick would appear like Thomas if she allowed him to sacrifice so much for her. And how could Nick ever live with that? Even if he could, she couldn't. And Charity would turn over in her grave.

She and Nick had married to protect the *kinner* from suffering as their mother had—not to repeat the same mistake. They hadn't fixed a thing. All they'd accomplished was to make everything worse. And it was her fault for putting the burden on Nick to find a solution. She'd been selfish, not wanting to leave, and pushed Nick to figure everything out. And now Nick was still trying by letting the farm go for her.

When she thought of it that way, Fern

sounded as self-centered as she'd always believed Thomas's current wife to be. What a terrible revelation.

Her stomach churned as she went through the motions of packing the laundry and sacking the potatoes to put into the wagon. She readied Sadie Mae for the ride back to the Weavers', determined to figure out how to undo the consequences of her selfishness before it was too late.

Chapter Twelve

A knock rapped at the store's front door as Nick prepared the register before opening time on Friday morning. He retrieved his keys and shut the cash drawer. He often opened early to waiting customers, only it was Eli on the other side of the glass door this morning.

Nick unlocked the door and opened it for his brother, who entered with a wide grin. "I have some important news for you. Looks like we can hold your house-raising day Tuesday after next. Seems folks are itching for a big community frolic. It's been a long time since we've done anything of the sort, and they are all eager to help. Ada getting the cottage back came as a relief to our church people, but they still want to see right done by you."

This was the Amish way, but still humbling

as the recipient of such generosity and concern. Nick felt he ought to pay something for the labor, but knew no one would accept it. Offering them money would be an insult to his Amish neighbors. He'd be sure to talk with Fern. Maybe they could give a sizable donation to the church benevolence fund to help someone else in their time of need.

"That is *wunderbar gut* news, Eli, the sooner, the better." He couldn't wait to tell Fern. She'd been somewhat pensive the past few days, and maybe this news would cheer her up. "You didn't happen to see Fern on your way in, did you? She was going to come water her flowers after taking Bethany to school."

"I believe I saw the back of her wagon going up toward Ada's when I pulled in the lot. If you want to be the first to tell her, you'd better not waste time. You know how fast this news will spread around the entire community." Eli grinned. "Sometimes, I believe we Amish still have cell phones and text messages beat for the speed of delivering information around here. The schoolchildren have a big softball game at lunch today. You know a good number of parents and grandparents will show up."

"*Ya*, true." Chatter at the ball game would quickly spread the news. "I'd like to see Bethany play, but I doubt I can get away from the store today."

"Tell you what, I'll send Zach over. I know you gave him the day off to help me get the farm ready for church this Sunday, but I can spare him a couple of hours this afternoon." Eli raised a hand to prevent an argument against his kind offer. "And take Fern with you. Sharon says she's been working herself to the bone between helping *Mamm*, Ada and us this week. She could use a break."

Eli had a kind heart. He could get bossy, but his intentions came from a place of concern. "*Denki*, Eli."

His brother nodded and headed back out the door to leave. A few seconds later, the bell above the door jingled. Eli held the door slightly ajar and poked his head through the narrow opening. "Fern's coming down the lane." And with a wink, he disappeared again.

Nick shook his head and chuckled. Who needed text messages, indeed.

Following behind Eli, he walked around the side of the building to make sure the watering hose was hooked up for Fern. By the time he'd hauled it up to the flower bed at the sign, she'd come up behind him.

Her green dress was fresh and clean, and

her hair smooth and neat. But the dark circles under her eyes hinted she didn't feel as ready for the day as she otherwise appeared. Eli had been right.

She stood beside him and reached for the nozzle end of the hose. "You didn't have to do this."

"You're welcome." He bumped his shoulder against hers and smiled at her. "Eli stopped by with some news you'll be happy to hear."

She looked directly at him then. "I saw him leaving. What did he say?"

"Folks are willing to have the house raising already." Retelling the news himself made the excitement of it all the more real to him. "Tuesday after next."

He waited for her response, but none came. Her gaze dropped to the ground and then to her flowers. She turned the nozzle head and aimed a steady spray at the base of the plants. Lines across her forehead deepened and her brow pinched together.

This was not the reaction he'd imagined. The news was supposed to relieve her, not burden her more. Nick scratched his head, then explained further.

"We can move out of *Mamm* and *Dat*'s house sooner now. Probably before the end of the summer. The *kinner* can get used to a new routine before school begins again in the fall. You'll be closer to Ada again. It will take some of the burden off of you." Nick searched his brain for more reasons to give her that this was a positive development. He hadn't expected that he'd need to. And she still wasn't reacting favorably—or at all. Was she that tired?

"Fern? What is wrong?"

She shifted the hose to spray a different section, then glanced sideways at him. "You don't have to do this for me. I… I don't *want* you to do it for me."

He didn't know what she was talking about or why she'd say such a thing. She sounded like the old, shy Fern who'd pulled away from the world after the fire. Somehow that riled him. "Well, it's too late to change our minds now. The whole community has rallied for this. For us, Fern."

She flipped the water nozzle off, dropped it at her feet and spun to face him. Her brown eyes blazed with anything but shyness. An intense battle waged behind them as she chose her words carefully.

Nick braced himself. He couldn't recall ever having a real argument with Fern before. The muscles in the back of his neck tensed. One was coming now, for sure, and he was oddly glad for it if it meant she wasn't going to shut him out.

"I'm tired of everyone's pity. And I don't want yours, either. We both made our promises to Charity so that the *kinner* don't suffer the way she did. That's why we got married, and we need to keep it that way. Things have changed since we planned the addition to the store. We can buy the farm now, and we should. Everything can go back to the way you wanted it in the first place."

Her words stung. He was trying to show her he cared. That their future was important to him. "I don't want the same thing anymore. And I don't believe that you do, either. That's what has changed. The *kinner* aren't suffering, Fern, and you know it. They are happy, well content and loved. They don't even miss the farm." And neither did he, he realized. For sure, he'd mourned when they'd left the place, but it was Charity he'd grieved again, not the farm. In truth, the farm had never felt like his own. It was Ada's—or so he thought—and would have become Charity's someday. He'd been grateful for it, but without Charity the purpose of it was gone, too.

Fern's lip trembled. "But we promised her."

"Fern, you are keeping your promise." If anyone wasn't fulfilling their end of the bargain, it was him—not her. How could he set her mind at ease that she was doing right by her cousin's memory? "Bethany and Josh will be happy wherever we provide them a stable and loving home. Of course, I mourned the loss of it. But it's dirt, Fern. Dirt and stone. Wood and nails. I don't want it at the cost of our future."

She studied him. Her eyes were intent on his face, assessing whether to believe him. For a second, her shoulders relaxed, as if she'd decided he meant what he said, but then her features clouded again with more worry.

"There's the trouble. You said you wanted to build the new house for me, and Thomas sure thinks I'm the reason that you're doing this. So will everyone else with the way he explains it. If you're concerned what people will think about halting the house raising, imagine what they'll think when Thomas spreads his tales. They already pity me, but they'll pity you more…for making such a big sacrifice for my sake. As if marrying me wasn't enough."

"What does that mean?" Marrying her was *not* enough, not until he could truly make her his *frau* instead of a nanny for his *kinner*. And she was as good as ever at clarifying that she wasn't interested in making the switch. Before she could sputter some insulting answer to his first question, he blurted out his next. "How do you know what Thomas thinks?"

"He came by the cottage after you spoke with him the other day." Her answer was curt. He waited for more explanation, but she wasn't forthcoming with the details.

"And?" Nick ground his teeth. More times than not, something Thomas said caused trouble between him and Charity, always because time with her *dat* left Charity feeling badly about herself. Now he'd gotten to Fern. "Do you really think we should continue to line Thomas's pockets for a piece of land? What did he say that has you feeling guilty about the farm?"

Nick couldn't help but wonder what made the man so desperate for cash that he'd bully Fern over this. And enough so that she'd lost sleep over whatever he'd said, which explained the dark circles under her eyes. "It's not so much what he said. It's the fact that I don't want us to repeat his mistakes."

"By building a home onto the store?" Nick attempted to unravel the logic behind her conclusion when a shiny red convertible pulled into a parking spot right in front of the store entrance. "I'm sorry but that doesn't make sense to me."

She released a breath as if getting ready to explain a simple problem to a child, when the bang of car doors jerked her attention to the store where two young women had gotten out and were climbing the stairs to the door. "Is anyone else inside?"

"*Nay*, but I'm sure they'll take a while before they want to check out." Still, he couldn't finish this conversation now. They were in a stalemate, anyway, and more likely to do damage than solve anything.

Attempting to moderate his tone of voice to something akin to pleasant, he changed the subject. "Eli also mentioned the softball game at the school this afternoon. Zach is coming over to cover for me. We could go together if you'd like."

She nodded. It wasn't exactly a reassuring delighted kind of agreement, but it was a yes, nonetheless. He'd take it.

"I can walk up to Ada's around lunchtime."

She picked the water hose up from where it had fallen to the ground. "I can come back here with the wagon to save time."

"*Denki*, that will be helpful." He wanted to

tell her not to worry about whatever Thomas had said but knew such a thing was easier said than done. Yet he hated the fact that she'd fretted over it all week. Whatever was going on in that sensitive heart of hers was tempting her away from all the progress they'd made.

"Fern. I'm sorry we can't finish talking now. We'll work this out." He didn't want to leave her there, thinking he was still angry. Confused and frustrated, *ya*, but his anger would pass. "I'll see you around noon, then?"

She gave him a simple nod and returned to watering her flowers, so he headed back to the store and his customers.

When he'd told Eli the sooner the better to get this house built, he hadn't known just how true a statement it was. In fact, sooner might not be soon enough. Fern's reaction made him wonder whether he'd been completely wrong about what would make her happy. He may have ruined their chance at a new start already.

If she really wanted the farm that badly, he'd agree, if it was only his dreams for their future going down the drain to settle in the past. But he still wasn't convinced that was what she truly wanted.

With a grip on the door handle, ready to open it, Nick paused long enough to say a prayer. Releasing matters beyond his control to the Lord, he'd have to go about his work as best he was able until he could speak more with Fern later. He prayed for one more chance.

Nick sure had dug his heels in this time. Fern knew how much he loved to solve a problem, as well as how good he was about seeing a solution through to its end, and yet she hadn't anticipated his stubborn refusal to buy the farm. Although she couldn't much blame him for not wanting to give Thomas more money after all her *grossmammi* had already put down on the farm in good faith.

But nothing he said alleviated the guilt that had pricked and festered like an imbedded splinter in her heart since she spoke with Thomas the other day. And the only explanation for Nick's unwillingness to go back to their original bargain was pure stubbornness. And she had no idea what exactly he was so stubbornly defending.

Fern had told Nick point-blank that the new house wasn't going to make her happy, and he still wasn't backing down.

He didn't believe her. Or at least he didn't believe her point was valid. She'd heard his skepticism. And he was going to insist on this move that Thomas would tell everyone proved Nick was just like him, doing their husbandly duty to satisfy their new wives.

She almost didn't care anymore. At least she hadn't until her temper cooled as she nearly drowned the flowers. Fighting against Nick was exhausting and he kept breaking down all her defenses. Leaving the store to walk back to *Grossmammi*'s cottage, Fern was more confused than ever.

She realized that stopping the house construction plans at this point wasn't practical or sensible. Her promise had been to love the *kinner*, which she couldn't stop doing if she tried. And Nick was right about Bethany and Josh being happy and loved.

The real problem was that she did care— maybe too much—about what people would say and think. With so many marks against her in other people's minds, she didn't believe she could bear another one. First the fire made her unfit for marriage. Not only was she scarred, but she was too irresponsible. And now, she knew they pitied her even more because Nick married her out of necessity. Now, to have Thomas's wagging tongue compare her to his greedy wife and Nick's choices to his own. *Nay*, it was too much.

As she crested the hill, she saw Josh and her grandmother in the yard. Josh was kicking a ball and *Grossmammi* was on the porch watching him and shelling the peas Fern had brought from her *mamm*'s garden.

Josh ran toward her. "Did you see? Did you see what I can do? Watch."

His little legs double-timed back to the purple bouncy ball, which he threw straight up into the air. As it fell, he maneuvered underneath and popped it back up with his head, sending it soaring into the rosebushes.

"He says he's going to play volleyball as *well* as Bethany plays softball." There was a chuckle in *Grossmammi*'s voice as she called over to Fern. "At least that rubber ball won't smash any windows."

They don't even miss the farm. Bethany and Josh will be happy wherever we provide them a stable and loving home.

Nick was right about that. Fern blew out a pent-up breath.

"What's bothering you, *Liebling*?" *Grossmammi* called to her using the affectionate term reserved mostly for children. She was still her grandmother's little girl when something was wrong. "*Kumm* and sit."

Fern joined her grandmother on the porch

and gathered a pile of peas in her lap to help snap. *Grossmammi* watched her, waiting for Fern to start the conversation. Fern knew the tactic. Ada would wait and just let her spill out whatever trouble was on her mind.

Only Fern was exhausted from the worries that had kept her from sleeping and eating well all week. *Nay*, she'd prefer to take a break from them before seeing Nick again, and just sit here and shell peas in peace.

"Eli has set the date for the house raising. Tuesday next." There. She did a decent job of sounding unbothered, but she watched to see if she'd convinced her grandmother everything was fine.

No reaction.

Peas continued to drop from the open shells in *Grossmammi*'s aged hands down to the half-filled bowl at her feet.

"I suppose you know I suggested using my savings to buy the farm."

Only a nod.

"Nick won't agree to giving Thomas another dollar."

At least that comment sparked the raise of an eyebrow. Then the corners of her grand-mother's mouth twitched with a smile.

That surprised Fern. "I thought you'd like

for us to get the farm, after all the years and money you invested in it. You sacrificed more than any of us ever knew trying to give Charity her heritage."

The heritage Thomas stole once from his daughter and now again from his grandchildren.

Grossmammi leaned forward. The bright green pod in her fingers cracked open, and she pushed her thumb along the inside length, releasing the peas into the bowl at her feet. "There's not much holding those little peas to their shell, but sometimes they still need a push to let loose."

She sat back against the seat and looked Fern in the eye. "Same as people can be. Stuck. Not much keeping 'em from where *Gott* wants them to go, yet they need a little push in the right direction. They get all comfortable where they're at and see no reason to change." She glanced down at the pot and chuckled. "Course, *Gott* ain't gonna eat us, like we're going to do to those peas. I might not have picked the best example, but the point is that He won't lose us, any more than I'll let those peas roll outta my sight. I've got plans for them. And *Gott*'s got plans for us. You have to know when it's time to let go and trust Him to catch you."

Grossmammi held up another open pod filled with ripe peas. "Now look." She shook it and a few plunked into the bowl while two clung tight. "Pretend like one of those left hanging is you. What's got you stuck?"

Fern wasn't sure how to answer. *Stuck* was a good word for how she felt lately and she recalled her conversation with Thomas that *Grossmammi* had overheard earlier that week. Guilt had clung to her ever since.

"I guess I feel guilty that Nick is building a new house. At first, I didn't because we had no other choice. But now, we do. Everyone is always doing things to protect me, as if that fire turned me into glass. And building this house isn't necessary. *Grossmammi*, I can't let Nick do something that makes him look bad... and me selfish."

Her grandmother leaned against the back of her chair with her hands folded in her lap. "If you were made of glass, perhaps you'd see things more clearly. And maybe Nick deserves a little more faith than you're giving him."

"I don't mean it's Nick who's at fault. It's me. The plans for that house are perfect. And all the effort he made for my sake, well, I felt so...so cared for. And I was excited about living there." Many evenings—before Thomas showed up—she'd fallen asleep with thoughts of the four of them in that house and all the memories they'd make. "It's a selfish dream, *Grossmammi*." Even as she spoke the words, she felt the tight tentacles of guilt squeeze her heart.

"Now, that's Thomas Miller's own guilt spilling over to you. He's made you believe you're as selfish as his own wife. She didn't want him to give Charity the farm outright, which he'd planned to do as recompense for leaving her here with me. And now that Charity is gone, his wife insists it is unfair for Bethany and Josh to get the farm without her grandchildren getting more money from it, as well.

"While I was down in the valley, I learned a few things about Thomas. Things I never knew about his situation. Fact is, we rarely know why a person does the things they do. Only *Gott* knows for sure. That's when I realized that I had to stop reliving in my mind how much he hurt Charity. There's no sense in keeping the pain going. Hasn't there been enough hurting already over it?"

"Ya." Fern shook her head. "More than enough."

"What Thomas says and does only has the power you allow. I won't let it invade my thoughts and rule my heart, not anymore. And you shouldn't, either."

Ach, how nice it would be to be free of worry over what other people thought. But even if she ignored all of that, Nick had still promised not to let the *kinner* forget their *mamm*.

All of his attention might make her heart flutter, and his talk of a new start might raise her hopes for the love of her dreams, but she was still bound by her promise. And to keep it, she had to make sure that he kept his.

Chapter Thirteen

Nick pulled himself up into the wagon after Fern arrived, right on time to go to the ball game at the Amish school. Taking the reins, he glanced over at Fern and Josh, who wiggled his way between them.

"Hey now." Nick gave a playful tug on Josh's suspenders. "Look at you taking the best spot."

Josh turned his face up to look at Nick from his seat on the wagon bench and nestled even closer to Fern's side, effectively pushing her farther away from Nick.

"I reckon I'll let you sit between us this time. Just don't forget I get first dibs on that position." Nick winked, and Fern's cheeks turned rosy.

The wagon lurched as Sadie Mae pulled them forward. *Ya*, he was pouring it on thick, but he was running out of time to win Fern over.

Josh kicked his legs back and forth. "Let's go faster."

Nick couldn't help but chuckle. "You must be ready to see your sister knock that ball into next Tuesday."

Josh scratched his head. "Where's Tuesday?"

This time it was Fern who laughed. "He looks like you when he does that?"

"What? Scratching his head? He's more like you, I think. You never get my jokes, either."

"Did you tell us a joke, *Dat*?"

Fern held a hand across her midsection and sputtered before releasing a full-out laugh.

"What's so funny, and where's Tuesday?"

"It's just an expression, Josh. Your *dat* means Bethany is a real *gut* batter."

"Oh, *ya*! She's better than Jeremiah Glick. I heard him say they pitched the ball easy to her or else she couldn't hit home runs like that. The other boys said he was just jealous, and I ran over his foot and stomped real hard."

"Joshua." The mortification on Fern's face quickly deflated the proud swell of Josh's chest. "We do not solve our disagreements by losing our tempers or hurting others."

Nick couldn't help feeling for his son. There was no greater punishment for a little boy than knowing he'd disappointed his *mamm*. But Fern was right to correct his behavior. "Listen to your *mamm*, *sohn*. She is right. And think about how you will handle something like that next time without reacting in anger."

"Jeremiah lied." Josh crossed his arms against his chest with a huff. "If I lied, I'd be in big trouble."

"*Ya*, but when we punish you for wrong, it is because we love you and know you must learn to do right, not because we are angry with you." Nick tried to think of an example. "Remember when you thought it was a *gut* idea to play with Fern's eggs... I mean *Mamm*'s eggs."

His little head hung low. Fern squirmed a bit in her seat, too. Maybe he shouldn't have brought it back up. "I don't mean to remind you of it to make you feel bad. You're already forgiven for that. I just want you to know that all of us have trouble with anger. Did you know I was angry when I came down and saw that mess of eggs all over the kitchen?"

He shook his head.

"Did I stomp on your toes or yell at you?"

"*Nay*." His eyes rounded at the thought.

"I was angry, but I had to work out what to do with those feelings before I disciplined you. If I had reacted while still angry, I would probably do the wrong thing. In fact, my wrong would be greater than yours because you are a child. You are still learning, but I am a grown man who knows better."

Fern looked over the top of Josh's head and gave Nick a slow smile, the kind a mother sent her husband to say he'd done well, and he felt the approval of it down to his bones.

"Jeremiah should have to scrub the floor," Josh proclaimed, then leaned back against Fern's side. She bit her lower lip to hold in a laugh.

Nick knew his track record was far from perfect. He disliked those memories as much as Josh hated remembering the egg incident. "I lose my temper, though, sometimes, don't I?"

"But you say sorry, and I forgive you."

"And you lost your temper with Jeremiah. What should you do?" Fern prodded.

Josh scrunched up his nose. "Say sorry."

The rest of the ride to the school was short. Josh caught sight of his sister and took off in her direction as soon as it was safe to jump from the wagon. Nick tied Sadie Mae to a post and came around to help Fern.

She placed her hand in his for balance as she hopped from the side of the wagon to stand beside him. Reluctantly, he let go of her hand, knowing a public display would embarrass her.

As they fell into stride with one another and headed to the play area at the back of the school, he tilted his head toward hers. "We make a *fine* team, you and I."

"He's a *gut* boy." She gazed toward the children. "I cannot take credit."

"Hmm." Nick wasn't up for another disagreement today. Still, he knew Josh needed Fern, and Nick never could have raised either child so well without her. He didn't know why she refused the compliment or the connection between them, but he wouldn't push it.

"Nick." Fern pulled him to a stop. Looking around them before she spoke, her voice was quiet, although no one was within at least ten yards of where they stood. Her brown eyes glistened. "I understand allowing Josh, and even Bethany, to call me *Mamm*. But when you refer to me...with the position that belongs to Charity..." Her voice descended to almost inaudible before picking back up again with more fervor. "It's like you've suddenly turned your back on the promises we made to her. I don't want to be the reason you replace her."

Fern stared at him, waiting for his answer, for what may have been the most uncomfortable minute of his life. She may as well have stabbed him straight through the heart. He thought navigating through life with young *kinner* and no wife was difficult, but working through this marriage with Fern was harder still. And all because he…

He loved her.

But for sure and certain, he couldn't tell her that right now.

"You're right. You are not Charity." Not by any stretch of the imagination. He had adored his first wife, but he had no desire to replicate her. "Don't accuse me of wanting you to be her, either, because I do not. I want you to be you, Fern. That is all I have ever wanted. And I cannot raise my son to do right without showing you the respect you deserve. You are *mamm* to him. And when I speak to him, I will respect that."

The fire in her eyes extinguished, and she looked down at her feet. He hadn't intended to scold. He tugged at the neck of his shirt. The afternoon had become unpleasantly hot and humid.

He sighed. "Do you still want to join the others?"

"Of course." She straightened her shoulders. "Bethany will be glad to see us here."

Maybe he was foolish to hope that Fern would ever see this marriage as more than a way to keep her promise to care for the *kinner*. She loved them, no doubt. He simply might have misjudged that she had ever once loved him.

And believing he could woo her to love him now… He might have to concede that as a lost cause, after all.

The gathering was informal. Parents and a few grandparents grouped in clusters behind home base. The teacher had brought out a few chairs for the older folk and set up a table with paper cups and gallon jugs of water and lemonade.

With the children divided into teams, fairly equal in their distribution of ages, the game was meant to inspire teamwork more rather than competition. Once the game began, Fern knew Nick would do his best not to show too much favoritism, but he never really fooled anyone about who his favorite player was.

And despite her current aggravation, she knew she'd find it endearing. Why did he have to be so likable? It was maddening. Not to mention how often he had to be right. She couldn't very well argue against him showing her respect with the *kinner*.

His method of teaching Josh proved what she already knew about Nick. He was a *gut* and kind father. But she was absolutely determined not to let his flirting wear her down further.

"There they are." Fern pointed across to the other side of home base where she'd caught sight of Bethany and Josh. A few steps closer and what she saw made her pause. "Thomas is talking to them."

"Well, he is their *grossdaddi.*" Nick never had used the more intimate term *dawdi* for Thomas with the *kinner.* And Thomas had never been around Bethany or Josh enough for them to refer to him with a name of their own choosing, like all the Weaver grandkids called his *dat Dawdi* Dan.

"I know that." Fern's mouth drew into a straight line. "It was just unexpected."

"*Ya.* That it is." He sounded more serious than he had a moment earlier and probably assumed she hadn't caught his joking tone. She felt a little snippy behaving as though she wasn't amused. But how else was she to keep him from knocking down her defenses before she found a way to make him understand why they had to keep their bargain the way they had planned?

By the time they reached the children,

Thomas had moved on to speak with someone else and some of the tension in her shoulders released.

As the other school-age children began either heading to the outfield or lining up to bat, Bethany looked up to Nick. "*Grossdaddi* said he hoped the farm could stay in our family after all. What does that mean? I thought we were going to live above the store. Me and Josh want to live at the store, don't we?" She tugged on her little brother's arm. "Right, Josh?"

"Uh-huh." Josh mumbled around a lollipop far too big for his mouth. "He gabe me dis."

"Josh would agree with anything you said, Bethany." Nick cast a questioning glance at Fern. He couldn't think she'd go behind his back, especially about this. Could he?

Fern raised both palms up. "I have no idea."

Nick patted Bethany on the shoulder. "I don't know what Thomas meant, either, but there's no need to worry. And, it looks like it's time to line up. Go get 'em." He winked at her before she ran off to join her team, then heaved Josh, sticky fingers and all, up on his shoulders to watch the game begin.

"Does he look happy up there?" Nick asked her, knowing full well how thrilled Josh was from his giggles.

She refused to answer. Because the next thing was to make her admit she'd heard Bethany say how much she wanted to live above the store. Then he'd believe he'd proved his whole point that she was doing just fine keeping her promise.

"I think I need a drink." She stepped sideways in the direction of the refreshment table. "Bethany's teacher is over there, too. I've been meaning to talk to her."

A victory smile spread across Nick's face. Spinning on her heel, she strode directly away from him. Maddening. That's what Nick Weaver was. A strong sympathy with Josh overcame her. Jeremiah Glick wasn't the only one who could use a *gut* foot-stomping.

Only Nick wasn't lying. His point was valid, which frustrated her more.

Reaching the table, she gulped down the first glass of water available. The cool trickle was just what she needed. She couldn't recall the last time she'd gotten so bent out of shape. As her pulse eased back to normal, she wondered what exactly Thomas had meant about keeping the farm in the family.

The only explanation that came to mind was that he was using the children to manipulate Nick into doing as he wanted. If he was, that sure backfired on him. Nick was more stubborn than to let a little manipulation change his mind. Thomas ought to know better. And now that she knew the *kinner* didn't want to return to the farm, Fern couldn't very well argue in favor of it, either.

Just then, she caught Nick looking at her from across the way. Or he caught her staring at him the whole time she'd been lost in her thoughts—ones he might be attempting to read. Only she couldn't really make out his expression, and she wasn't ready to go discuss all of this with him again, either.

She turned to find the schoolteacher, but saw Cassie instead. She was emptying a box filled with cookies and whoopie pies, and arranging the treats at the other end of the table. Cassie looked up at Fern and tilted her head with a little swing to suggest Fern come closer, so Fern walked to where she was standing.

"I don't want to spread any rumors, but it was Thomas himself who said something to me. He said he'd be going back home to the valley today…" Cassie leaned closer to Fern, her eyes wide and her voice soft. "…because he is meeting with Martin about the farm." Cassie swallowed and her eyes darted around them. "I wouldn't want to call anyone a liar. But…it's hard to believe."

If anyone would want to believe that Martin intended to return to Promise, Cassie would. Undoubtedly, she felt the same burst of hope Fern did about the possibility—and just as quickly discounted it. Martin hadn't given her any sign he desired to return home.

Unless Cassie knew more about what Martin was thinking than Fern did. "Did you see Martin when he was here?"

She blushed and looked down at the chocolate whoopie pie in her hands. "He slipped in the back of the store early one morning, but he didn't say anything about this."

That Martin sought Cassie out, and secretively, during his brief stay was a good indicator to Fern that Thomas was likely speaking the truth.

Cassie stalled, lost in thought, with the cookie still in her hands. Fern took it from her and placed it in the neat row Cassie had made with the rest of her baked goodies. Cassie looked up at her. "Do you think Martin might buy the farm and come back?"

Fern patted Cassie's empty hand. "I haven't heard anything about it. But you know how private Martin can be. I pray every day for his return if *Gott* wills it. We can hope this is the way He sees fit to answer *our* prayers." She knew Cassie desired the same, even if she was too shy to confess it. "Only time will tell."

Cassie nodded. "*Denki*, Fern."

If Martin was indeed considering the purchase of Thomas's land, then Fern's insistence on buying the farm would interfere with the happiness of even more people she loved. Better to be thought selfish by those who didn't understand than to be truly selfish and hurt those she held dear.

She'd been forcing herself not to think about how much she'd also looked forward to living above the store. A ripple of pleasure ran up her spine, thinking how nice it would be to live there.

Ach, but a home of their own! How much harder it was going to make keeping her relationship with Nick as the friendship they'd both promised it should remain.

Poor Nick. A weight like lead plummeted to the pit of her stomach.

Irritated as she had been with him that day, she hated the sound of that more than *Poor Fern*. She may as well accept that was how it was going to be after she conceded to let the farm go.

Poor Nick, who gave up everything for Fern. In whispered conversations for the rest of their lives, she'd hear some version of the same tiresome song. *Grossmammi* may be able to ignore what other people said, but it all still made Fern's stomach churn.

Chapter Fourteen

Nick couldn't sleep.

Again.

Tossing the single top sheet to the side of the bed, he sat up. The light of a full moon spilled through the open window and illuminated his sparse room. He slipped on his trousers and pulled the suspenders over his shoulders. The night was warm. Since he wasn't going to sleep anyway, he may as well go sit under the stars rather than stare at a blank ceiling.

He didn't bother with shoes or a hat, just quietly snuck down the hall toward the kitchen. A shadow stretched long across the floor from the kitchen. He wondered who else was up at this hour. The dark silhouette moved, revealing the outline of a woman.

His suspicion confirmed as he entered the

room and saw who was standing at the sink with her back to him. "Fern?"

The sound of his voice startled her. She spun around with one hand over her heart and the other clinging to a glass. "Shh."

He wasn't sure if she was admonishing him or if it was just the sound of her surprise and relief mixed together. He went up beside her, so he could keep his voice low enough not to disturb the rest of the household. "What are you doing?"

"I was hot and thirsty. I needed a cold drink." She held up the glass in her defense, and he smelled the minty-sweet aroma of his *mamm*'s iced meadow tea. Then her eyebrow rose. "What are you doing?"

"Couldn't sleep." He watched her relax her back against the counter. He wasn't sure in the low light, but she didn't appear ready to go to sleep, either. "I was going to sit outside for a while. See if that helped."

She sipped her drink and hummed an amused sound over the rim of her cup. "Still sneaking out to sleep under a tree at your age?"

"It's not like we're ancient." He pretended to be insulted, then had an idea. "Want to join me?"

"Depends." She glanced up at him before

turning to place her empty glass in the sink. "Whether we can get along or if we'll just argue."

"Now you are talking as if I'm a child. I like that better than as an old man, but you really should make up your mind." He was teasing, but her sigh made him wonder if she thought he was still arguing with her instead. "Fern, I don't want to argue, either. I was joking."

"I know. I actually got that this time. It is impossible to stay mad at you, Nick Weaver." She brushed her hands down the length of her nightgown. "But I can't go outside like this."

"It's one a.m., Fern, no one will see us. I can barely see you myself." He looked at the length of fabric that stretched from her collarbone all the way to the top of her feet. "I really don't think there's anything to worry about. And no wonder you're hot." He added the last bit without thinking.

Another sigh. "Fine."

"*Kumm*, then." He took her hand. "It will be cooler outside, and maybe we'll even catch a breeze."

He headed for the apple orchard where his *dat* allowed the grass to grow longer, creating a much more comfortable spot for lying down to stargaze. As he bent down to run his hands over the grass and clear any twigs or debris that would poke and pinch them, Fern stifled a yawn.

"Would you rather go back to bed?"

"*Nay*, not yet. It is much more comfortable out here. But tomorrow is going to be a long day if we don't get some sleep."

How well he knew it. This wasn't his first go-round with a sleepless night.

Determined not to bring up all the worries that kept him awake, he mentioned the surrounding sounds instead. An owl hooted and a hunting dog howled in the distance. They admired the Milky Way, though somewhat dimmed by the full moon. Still, way up here on the mountain with almost no artificial light anywhere nearby, the constellations were visible, even tonight.

He'd hoped coming outside would relax him, and he found with Fern by his side he was even more so, which only made him more determined to find a way to keep the peace between them.

Earlier in the evening, when Fern had told him what Thomas had said to Cassie, she'd sounded so defeated. He knew she was genuinely happy for her brother and hopeful of his return home, but she couldn't hide her worry from him. No matter what she said about understanding that they needed to let the farm go and live above the store, he couldn't do so if it made her miserable.

He turned his head and caught her in an openmouthed yawn. Her head lolled to face him. "I believe I could sleep better out here, but I'll have to go inside soon."

She was as relaxed as he was. And he was more determined than ever to solve whatever it was that kept coming between them.

If it came to it, his *dat* had agreed they could stay here as long as necessary. All Nick needed was a little more time. He hoped.

When Fern's yawns began to come more frequently, he walked her back to the house. He didn't want their time together to end, especially since he'd still probably not sleep. But he was thankful for the sweet hour or so alone with Fern, with no talk of farms or house raisings, or even of the *kinner*.

"I'm glad you joined me, Fern. I hope you won't be too tired tomorrow."

"I'm glad, too." Her mouth opened wide, and she covered it with her palm.

"Go on, then. I'll see you in the morning."

Her hand dropped to her side, and her feet

shuffled with fatigue as she slipped through the door into her bedroom.

He'd planned to go back outside alone, but suddenly he felt relaxed and headed to his bed instead. His head sank down into the feathery pillow, and he closed his eyes. Soon, he was enveloped by images of the stars through the shadows of tree limbs and the scents of summer grass and Fern's lavender soap.

Around dawn, a rooster's crow woke him before he had another conscious thought. He hadn't slept so well in a very long time.

And all he knew was that whatever was on today's agenda, it had to include working things out with Fern.

His morning routine went a lot faster since he'd gotten some rest, and he entered the kitchen to find it empty, except for the two half-gallon jugs of covered milk in an ice bath on the counter. His *dat* had already milked this morning, but must have gone back out to feed the horses. Nick stoked the fire to prepare the *kaffi* they'd all be wanting soon. The only problem was that at his parents' house, Fern hadn't prepared the pot for him like she used to do.

He fumbled around for the canister where his *mamm* kept the ground beans and sent the tin lid skidding across the countertop before it plunked onto the floor.

"Here." His *mamm* stood over him as he reached down to grab the cover lying at his feet. "I better make the *kaffi*, or else no one will be able to drink it." She held out her hand for the container.

"Gladly." He rested the lid back on top and handed it to her. "Can I do something else?"

"Not before you have your *kaffi*," she teased. "Have a seat and keep me company. We don't get many opportunities to talk, just you and me."

Why did Nick sense that she had something specific to say to him, rather than an ordinary chat? She put the percolator on the stove, then pulled out a chair to sit with him.

"Fern is usually out here before I am, so let's get to the point while we are alone." His *mamm* rarely beat around the bush on any subject, so Nick couldn't help the grin sneaking across his face. "This isn't a joking matter, son. You've got a situation on your hands. And I have to say it is all of your own making, too. Fern is not as complicated to figure out as you are making this."

Fern was the most complicated woman Nick knew. Except for maybe Ada. And his *mamm*.

Okay, well, maybe not the most difficult to predict, but still… If his *mamm* had it all figured out, he'd be more than happy to hear it.

"Love her. That's all you have to do. Everything else will fall into place if your words *and* your actions show her that she is loved. It's as simple as that."

"*Mamm*, that's what I've been doing…trying to do…" She made it sound so simple. "The thing is…" Nick was cut short by the stern expression on his *mamm*'s face.

"*Gut mariye*, Fern." She spoke over his head as Fern entered the kitchen through the door behind him. "The *kaffi* is almost ready. And Nick was just saying how he thought he'd go get the eggs for you this morning. Won't you join me?"

Fern came up beside him and gave him a pointed look. "Did Nick make it?"

"Very funny. *Mamm* rescued us all and made it." He knew his cue to leave. Besides the fact that it was Bethany's job to gather the eggs, his *mamm* clearly had a speech waiting for Fern, too, luring her in with the same invitation she'd given him minutes ago.

He stood to leave. "Sorry you didn't get the luxury of drinking my *kaffi*, but I can burn the bacon for you when I return."

He closed his eyes. Why did he keep making that idiotic joke? He'd probably upset Fern again with the reminder of the kitchen fire she'd started, although not with bacon, thankfully.

"Fern." He began an apology and opened his eyes.

To his surprise, her eyes sparkled, and she coughed back a laugh. "It would be *wunderbar* of you to cook for me, Nick. I am a bit tired this morning." She gave him a cheeky half grin and plopped down in the chair. "We can wait."

"Just remember that you asked for it," he teased back, and his *mamm* glanced between the two of them and raised her hands heavenward as if pleading for help.

Nick made quick strides across the room for a hasty retreat out the side door, before he did accidentally say something to ruin the easy banter between them that had spilled over from the night before.

He wondered what advice his *mamm* was about to give Fern. That was one pitfall about their living arrangement, the one he'd most wanted to rectify. He and Fern had so few opportunities to work things out themselves, even if their families meant well. But that was unlikely to change anytime soon now.

His *mamm* was right about one thing. Nick had made a mess of things with Fern. And a few jokes weren't going to fix it. Still, the fact that he and Fern could share a private joke in the middle of everything had to be some sign of hope, didn't it? *Gott* knew he needed one.

Rhoda poured two steaming mugs of hot *kaffi* and ladled a dollop of thick fresh cream into one. With the spoon still in her hand, she looked at Fern. "Want some? I just scooped it off the milk Daniel brought in this morning, so it's nice and fresh."

Fern's mouth watered. Nothing could beat fresh cream. And her mother-in-law didn't really require a response. She knew how well Fern liked it and dropped a generous portion in the second cup before recovering the milk jar and returning it to the ice bath.

"We can put the milk away after we have our first cup." Rhoda came to the table and slid it across the smooth wooden tabletop to Fern. Not much came between Rhoda and her morning cup of *kaffi*.

"So," Rhoda stated after a few sips of her drink. "Daniel tells me that Nick spoke to him about staying here and renting the house above the store for a while."

The abrupt subject change caught Fern off guard. "What?"

"I'm not surprised that you don't know he's thinking about this. He was looking for advice, more than actually having made a decision. He feels staying here is the only option. Apparently, he spoke with your *dat* as well and confirmed that what you heard about the farm was true."

So, it wasn't a rumor. Fern's *dat* would know the truth of her brother's plans. "If my brother wants the farm, I'd never get in his way. Besides… The *kinner* made it plain they aren't in favor of returning to the farm, either.

"I told Nick so." On their way back from the ball game, she'd told him that she realized moving into the new house was their only option now. Why would he come up with this plan to rent the house and stay with his parents? "I think Nick must have talked to his *dat* about staying here and renting the space above the store before…before I agreed that we should let the farm go."

Rhoda shook her head. "*Nay*, he spoke to his *dat* just before they went to bed last night. Nick is a problem-solver. If you are still unhappy about moving into the new house, then he won't force you. And this is one way he thought he might be able to compromise."

"How thoughtful." Which, of course, Nick was. He might say the wrong thing sometimes, but he had a kind heart.

"*Ya*, but Fern, I told you because I wanted you to have a chance to consider this idea before Nick tells you about it. You are all welcome in our home anytime. I like having the *kinner* close. And I enjoy sharing the tasks of our everyday lives with you, too. And I can see the idea is something of a relief to you. Obviously, Nick knew it would be."

Fern sensed another *but* coming. Her momentary relief from hearing Nick's proposed solution dissolved like a cold sugary treat might on a hot day before you got the chance to enjoy it. And as much as she dreaded to hear why Rhoda appeared not to like the idea, she respected Nick's *mamm* and her opinion. She had to ask. "But you don't think it is a *gut* idea, do you?"

Rather than eagerly expressing her thoughts, as Rhoda usually would do, she sipped at her *kaffi* first. Then, leaning forward and placing a warm hand on top of Fern's rather chilled one, Rhoda spoke ever so gently.

"Please, consider carefully, Fern. You may

very well be choosing once and for all whether you want a husband or not. Do you want to go through life only for the sake of the *kinner*? Or is your heart's desire to be cherished and loved by a godly man who is committed to loving his *frau*? Because the longer the two of you maintain this unnatural distance between you, the less likely it is that you will ever overcome it.

"The choice is yours. No one, not even Nick, will decide for you."

Chapter Fifteen

Sunday morning dawned, revealing a light fog, which promised sunshine and a pleasant day to follow. And by the time the family were all ready for church, the sun had burned away the mist and a sky to match the bright blue of the men's shirts spread overhead without a cloud in sight.

As Fern tied the laces of Josh's shoes, Nick came up beside her. She looked up, first to Josh, whose head turned impatiently with his desire to run outside, and then much higher to Nick, who smiled down at her.

"What do you think? Should we walk to Eli's for service this morning, or would you prefer that we take the buggy?"

"Seems a shame to waste such a beautiful day enclosed in a buggy." She let go of Josh's foot and he disappeared out the door faster than she was able to stand up. "And the walk may help that one sit through the sermon."

"A walk it is." Nick grabbed his hat off the hook by the door, cupping the top of it in his hand as his arm relaxed beside his leg. With his other hand, he held the door open for her.

"Denki." Fern passed through the door, aware of his admiring glance as she went. She heard the door close behind them, as Nick leaned over her shoulder.

"You look nice this morning." He stepped beside her and propped his hat over his thick curls. "I like when you wear that color."

The royal blue shade was the same as almost every other Amish woman would wear to church that morning. Silly as the comment was, it warmed her to hear it. And she had to make an effort not to blush.

"Are you tempting me to be vain?" The attempt at a scold wasn't any stronger than the weakness in her knees when he winked back at her.

She decided to change the subject. "Should we wait for Rhoda and Daniel?"

He raised a brow to say he knew what she was doing. *"Nay.* They will drive to get there a little earlier, but we have plenty of time to walk and still be there to help with any last-minute details."

Still, he looked a little puffed up to her, knowing his flirtation had gotten to her. He thought he'd one-upped her, and she couldn't let it go.

"You're crooked." She made sure to sound as disapproving as possible and tugged to straighten his jacket. "See. Look, what a mess. Do I need to dress you like I do for Josh?" To make her point, she used both hands and smoothed away the smallest of wrinkles from his shirt, then looked up with the sternest expression she could pretend.

Only his gaze down to her hands and then to her face stilled her. She watched as he left at least a half-dozen replies unspoken, except in the spark of those deep blue eyes and the humorous twitch at his lips.

But in the end, he simply cleared his throat and said thank-you, calling the *kinner* to join them. And with her heart about to beat out of her chest, they began their walk to church.

Do you want to go through life only for the sake of the kinner? *Or is your heart's desire to be cherished and loved by a godly man who is committed to loving his* frau?

Her heart made its desire plain enough.

Maybe her choice to marry Nick hadn't been such a tremendous sacrifice, after all. Perhaps she'd merely been grasping one last frantic time at the dream that always eluded her. The dream walking in step with her even now, and the man to whom her heart tugged without mercy.

The choice is yours.

Had the time finally come when the only choice her heart ever wanted was finally hers for the taking?

Guilt latched on to her like a horse's bit that pulled her back to the old worn path it wanted to travel. Nick had made a promise…and she knew she couldn't live with being the reason he broke it.

Despite what *Grossmammi* and Rhoda thought, it wasn't that simple.

She considered what her *mamm* might say and wondered why she hadn't sought her *mamm*'s advice sooner. If she'd survived the embarrassingly personal talking-tos from both her grandmother and mother-in-law, then surely, she could muster enough courage to speak with her own *mamm* about this. And she would, soon.

Nick pulled out his handkerchief and wiped his forehead. The uphill hike to Eli's had him in a sweat. Of course, the way Fern had raised his blood pressure at the start contributed a good bit to his warmth.

She and the *kinner* had gone straight to the house, where they'd stay until time to file into the barn for the church service. He followed the sound of male voices around the side of the barn and found Eli, along with their *dat*, Naaman Burkholder and Ezekiel Beiler huddled in a discussion. They didn't seem to notice he'd come up on them.

"Gut mariye." He interrupted to avoid eavesdropping. "Just wondering where you might need my help."

Looking Nick's way, Eli motioned for him to join them. "All that's left to be done is for the *kinner* to retrieve the hymnals from the church wagon."

They'd know the job was to be done as they arrived, the same as it was every church Sunday. "Sorry I didn't get here sooner to help."

Eli waved off the apology.

Naaman, in his role as their bishop, caught him up on the conversation. "You are just in time. I was telling your *dat* and Ezekiel that we've heard from Thomas's bishop. Martin, along with the help of one of the Beachy ministers, has approached Thomas with an agreement to make peace between the two families. Thomas has agreed. And now the bishop wants to know if the arrangement is also agreeable with Ada and with you."

"But it is not my land." Nick turned to Ezekiel. "What matters is what Ada and your family find fair. I am not seeking anything from this." Although Fern was a Beiler, too. She'd been very sure that she wanted Martin to have the farm, especially if it brought him home. "I am certain Fern feels the same."

"I understand." Ezekiel clapped an affirming hold on Nick's shoulder. "You've never sought your own gain in this matter. But it is Thomas who made the request that you be included. As his late daughter's widower and father of two of his grandchildren, it is only right."

Ezekiel's hand dropped from Nick's shoulder, and he shifted his feet as he hesitated to go on. "I confess I've had little faith in Thomas Miller since the day he abandoned my niece right after my sister's funeral. Unlike my *frau*, who prayed for him through the years, I did not believe such prayers were worth the waste of breath."

Nick felt as near to tears as his new father-in-law sounded. He'd harbored similar thoughts himself.

For several seconds no one spoke, but then Ezekiel found his voice once again. "Bethany must've seen him on her way home from school one day. I don't know what she said, exactly, but it was a memory of Charity that reached down into the recesses of Thomas's heart. Somehow that combined with his interactions with you and my daughter, and for reasons I reckon only *Gott* knows, he found the will to do what he always knew he should.

"His desire is for it to go to Bethany and Josh, but he understands your desire to focus on the store." Ezekiel paused again. He was struggling to tell the tale, and yet Nick heard the underlying approval in his voice and felt Fern's *dat* understood Nick wanted what was best for his daughter.

"So, Martin has suggested a compromise." Nick's *dat* spoke up, seeming eager to get to the point or to help his friend and neighbor explain such an emotional topic for him. "Thomas will sign the deed over to Ada as promised, and the land can be held in a trust for the *kinner,* like the *Englisch* do, but overseen by the church rather than the courts. And if you still do not wish to live on the farm, then

Martin will lcase it from Ada, but the money will be held for Thomas's grandchildren, including those by his second wife."

Nick leaned his back against the outside barn wall and blew out a long breath. "And Ada agrees?"

"*Ya.*" Ezekiel nodded, then muttered, "Mostly. She doesn't want Martin to pay for a lease, but she accepts that he can do as he wishes with his money. Or, in her words, throw it to the wind. Otherwise, she is at peace knowing the land will go to Bethany and Josh equally when they are of age."

Nick rubbed at the back of his neck. "I don't know what to say."

"There is no cause for a hasty answer," Naaman spoke up. "We will keep all of this in strict confidence. You need not worry others will know of it before you are ready. Discuss this with your *frau*. Pray over it. And when you have reached an agreement with Fern, then you can let Eli or I know, and we will inform Thomas's bishop."

By the time Nick stood in line with the rest of the men for the procession into the service, he'd made some sense out of all he'd been told. He wondered what Charity would think. While he knew she was fully at peace in heaven with

Gott, he couldn't help but imagine that she'd approve. Thomas had failed to show her the concern a daughter longed for from her father, but he was trying now for her children.

And for that, she'd rejoice and be thankful. He ought to do the same.

He'd always thought that he'd forgiven Thomas, just couldn't trust him. But he couldn't call Thomas unrepentant any longer. The man deserved another chance.

The line in front of him shuffled forward. And as they rounded the corner, he saw the women filing in through the opposite door to the other side of the barn. He searched for Fern among them and saw her with Bethany on one side and Josh on the other.

His heart pounded as hard as it had when she'd fussed over the wrinkle in his shirt.

Ya, Thomas deserved another chance. *Gott* knew how many times Nick had begged for one for himself. He sent up a silent plea for one more.

After the service, Fern went with the women to bring out the food, while the children gathered up the bibles and Ausbund hymnals and the men set up tables and rearranged the church benches for lunch.

Soon she traversed back to the barn again with both arms laden with platters of lunch meats and sliced cheeses. Between her fingers she grasped the tops of bread bags for folks to make their sandwiches.

Dodging the young *kinner* at play, she wove her way to the long line of tables arranged for the food. Cassie came behind her with a tray filled with bowls of sandwich spreads and another with jars of pickled beets.

Everyone was hungry after the long service. And they had the meal down to a predictable efficiency to feed the gathering as quickly as possible with minimal effort. So long as everyone followed their part, the process moved like clockwork.

After arranging the trays of food along with the bread, Fern headed back to the house to retrieve her next load. At the entrance to the barn, she heard her name and looked to see who was calling her. Finding no one looking for her, she was about to step outside when she heard her name again. *Poor Fern.*

No one was calling for her. They were talking about her.

"I don't want to listen to this. We both have work to do."

"Don't get so high and mighty with me,

Cassie Weaver." Cassie tried to leave, but an arm pulled her back.

"Can you imagine?" the same female voice as before continued. "I hope no one ever forces one of us to marry a man who only needs a nanny for his *kinner*. And poor Nick, everyone knows he only married Fern because he had no other choice. No wonder he wants to leave the farm. You know he must still love Charity. Why else would he want an apartment over a store compared to a beautiful old farmhouse? I bet her memory haunts him. And that scar…"

"What do you know about anything, Nancy Burkholder? That is the meanest thing I ever heard you say!" Indignation filled Cassie's voice as her profile came into view. "Don't bother talking to me at all, if that's how you're going to be." Cassie stormed away from her friend and never even noticed Fern still half-hidden by the door frame.

Fern braved a step into the open where Nancy stood with her mouth wide open. But it wasn't Nancy who got her attention. *Nay*, it was Nick—his expression fiery—directly behind the girl whom she had heard gossiping.

Nancy came to her senses first among them, looking initially at Fern and then turning around to see Nick. She sputtered the start of some sort of apology, but Nick didn't remain long enough to hear her finish. When Nancy turned back around, Fern noticed the girl at least had the sense to appear frightened. "Fern, I..."

"Excuse me, Nancy, I need to go." Fern sprinted after her husband.

Doing so would only make tongues wag more. What did it matter? In all their lives, she'd never seen Nick so angry.

Chapter Sixteen

Naaman Burkholder ought to spare some of his sermonizing for that youngest daughter of his.

Nick fumed. He was alone behind his brother's smokehouse, attempting to collect his wits before returning to the lunch gathering.

He'd taken off in the opposite direction before he taught the bishop's daughter a much-needed lesson himself. Amazing what people had the nerve to say when they thought no one was listening. Cassie hadn't seen him, either, and yet she'd stood up for what was right. Where she'd gotten the gumption for a confrontation like that, he had to wonder.

All he could figure was that the comment about Fern had been her last straw. And now, she'd be upset until she and her friend made amends, even if she hadn't sounded like she cared if they ever did. Nick knew his tender-hearted niece better than that.

But worst of all, no one had known Fern was nearby. For a few seconds after she'd appeared through the door, he'd hoped she had missed the whole thing. But once she'd looked up at him, he knew she'd heard.

At first, Nancy's ignorant speech annoyed him. By the time she finished, he was roiling at a well-controlled slow boil, and then Cassie's defense distracted him. But one look at Fern, and he knew he couldn't handle the situation without regrets. He had to abandon the scene or else explode. And nothing good would come from that.

He hated to be so weak, but a man had to know his limits. Apparently, silly young women's loose tongues and wild imaginations were his. Although he couldn't say he'd ever paid them any attention before.

He wouldn't now, if not for Fern.

He wanted to tell her he didn't give one fig what Nancy or anyone else said.

But Fern cared.

He may not be the wisest man around, but he knew that if a man told a woman not to care about something, he'd only make the problem ten times worse. But that wasn't the reason he was standing back here, instead of in line for lunch. He could have walked away, brushed aside what Nancy had said, and gone to talk to the menfolk without thinking about it again until he could check on Fern.

That's how he'd normally handle something like this. But this time was different. This time, the realization that the gossip was his own fault hit him about ten strides after he walked away. *Everyone knows he only married Fern because he had no other choice.*

The horrible truth of Nancy's statement had struck him like a kick in the gut. That's when he'd kept on walking, to figure out what he was going to do about it.

Still short on answers, he heard his name and glanced around the side of the smokehouse to see Fern searching for him.

"Over here." He called to her and stepped out so she could find him.

"Are you *all right*?" She was closer to him now, and he could see the worry lines on her forehead.

"I'm not worried about myself."

"Well, I am." Her hands went to her hips. "I've never seen you like this. You scared me."

"Sorry." For so many things. "I didn't want to hang around and wring Nancy's neck."

He half expected the scolding she'd given Josh for stomping on Jeremiah's foot, but she snickered instead. "I'm sure she's not in any danger. But you're going to miss lunch."

He rubbed his stomach. "I doubt I'll starve. And I needed to think."

"I'm bothering you."

"*Nay.* You are not. I feel better seeing you." She tugged at her prayer *kapp*.

"Fern, don't do that." He reached up, placing his own hand between hers and the scar that puckered along that side of her neck. It was the first time he'd ever intentionally touched her there. Maybe the first time anyone had. He pressed the palm of his hand closer to her skin and stepped into the space between them. "The scar would never keep a man from wanting you. You don't need to cover it up, especially not with me. Please believe me."

"That's not what's bothering me." She sounded slightly breathless and stepped back from him, so that his hand dropped. "I was afraid living above the store would do this— make people feel sorry for you. I'm resigned to being *Poor Fern* forever. But *Poor Nick*—I can't bear it. Especially when it's all because of who I am."

"Who you are? Who you are, Fern, is not a problem. And certainly not a burden." The volume of his voice was rising with each word. He sucked in a deep breath for control.

"I know I need to worry less about what other people think...or say. I promise to try. But even if I ignore everyone else, I still have to live with what my own heart knows. And Nick, I know you married me because of your promise to Charity. You didn't have a choice. And no matter how much I wish that was different, it is the truth."

"It *was* the truth." At least he'd thought so at the time, but not anymore. That's what he needed to think about. What he needed to figure out how to explain—how it wasn't true anymore.

"And I am so sorry for it."

"You're sorry?"

"*Ya.* I had believed I was making a sacrifice. But now, I realize I really agreed to your proposal because... I never would have possessed the will to turn down what I had always wanted. Not like that. I didn't want you to be forced to marry me. But I wanted to marry you."

How he wished he still had her face in his hand. He'd kiss her now. But she was drifting farther away. He reached, but she was turning to go.

"We really can't stay back here. I need to get back to help and you will miss the men's turn to eat if we don't hurry."

The change of subject broke his train of thought, and he knew she'd done it on purpose.

He wanted to tell her he loved her, but not here, hiding behind his brother's smokehouse on a Sunday afternoon like a wayward child. He had to wait until he could do it right. And he wouldn't just tell her. *Nay*, he'd show her first. Somehow, he'd find a way so that she'd have no doubt he meant it.

She was already heading back. He caught up to her with a quick jog.

"Fern, wait, there's something important I need to tell you about Thomas."

She groaned.

And he couldn't blame her, even though the sound made him chuckle. "It's not bad and won't take long. I won't make you miss your turn in line for lunch, too. I'll even serve your plate myself."

"While you sneak some for yourself, I'm sure." She was smiling at him. "What's this about Thomas that won't sour our stomachs before we eat?"

* * *

A week after Nick shared the story of the peace offering Thomas had made, thinking about it still made Fern teary. They'd taken two days to pray over it, and then sent word of their acceptance of the resolution.

To her dying breath, Fern's cousin had believed her father was redeemable. And while Charity had done all in her power to spare her own children the kind of heartache she'd known, she hadn't been bitter against her *dat*.

Nay, Charity had understood forgiveness on a level Fern doubted she ever could. She imagined that even up in heaven, Charity was rejoicing. Thomas had come back to Promise to transfer the deed to Ada. And he'd made a genuine effort to get to know the *kinner*.

How thrilled Charity would be for Bethany and Josh to have the relationship with their grandfather that she had so longed for. Charity never cared about money or land. That was *Grossmammi*'s fight for her granddaughter. All her cousin ever wanted was her father's love.

Fern wiped away a tear and took a deep, steadying breath as she walked over to her parents' house.

Martin had arrived late the night before to help with the house raising in two days. She couldn't wait to hug him. After all the effort her brother had taken to make peace for their families, she didn't care if hugs made him squirm. He was going to get one, anyway.

If *Gott* had answered her *mamm*'s prayers for Thomas in such an amazing way, was it possible He might answer an almost impossible request for her?

In two days, their humble home above Weaver's Store would become a reality. Small as it may be, it would be home to those she held most dear in all the world. But she couldn't deny any longer that she wished with all her heart to make it fuller. To add more *kinner* and to grow old with Nick more deeply in love with each passing year.

But she'd practically spelled out how she felt to him. Hadn't she? Her confession that she had wanted to marry him seemed plain enough to her. She'd laid her heart bare to him. Granted, she hadn't given him a chance to respond at the time. She'd hurried away to spare herself the embarrassment if he didn't.

Still, he'd had ample opportunity over the past week but hadn't said a word more on the subject. Much less declared that he loved her. Of course, he'd been busy getting ready for the house raising.

But he couldn't be too busy to utter three little words. And all she needed was for him to mean them. That was it, though—the impossible request. She'd known so from the beginning. So why did she continue to allow herself to hope for a change?

Entering her parents' house through the back door, Fern walked into the kitchen, where her *mamm* sat alone at the table. Her graying head was bent as if in prayer and a Bible lay open in front of her. Hearing Fern, she looked up.

"I'm so glad you stopped by. Your *dat* and brother have gone to do some visiting, but I stayed home to rest."

Martin had gone visiting? Her reclusive brother had changed more than she thought. "I had hoped to see Martin."

"Maybe they will be back soon." Her *mamm* shrugged as if she couldn't know for sure.

"At least you and I can talk, since we almost never have a moment alone with each other." Fern pulled out a chair and sat across from her mother. "I have been wanting to speak with you."

Her *mamm* closed the Bible, then folded her hands together in her lap, ready to give her full attention to Fern. Her *mamm* was a good listener. She wasn't one to lecture; at most she only ever gave a gentle prod in the right direction.

And while *Grossmammi* and Rhoda had given Fern a lot to consider, she missed her *mamm*'s gentle manner. Fern twisted the corner of her apron between her fingers. But where to start?

"I don't think we've had a mother-to-daughter chat since your wedding." *Mamm* spared her from starting the conversation.

"*Ach*, *Mamm*, you know it is not a real marriage." Fern dropped the fabric in her hands and let them fall to her sides. "Nick tries to make me happy, but…"

Her *mamm*'s eyes clouded with worry. "Your *grossmammi* and *dat* would have pushed you and Nick into marriage much sooner. I held them back because I feared this."

"You knew he couldn't love me."

"*Nay*, I knew you were not ready to let him."

Did she hear that right? Her *mamm* thought Fern wasn't allowing Nick to love her. Fern shook her head.

"How about some tea and cookies?" Without waiting for an answer, her *mamm* put the kettle on and brought a plate of oatmeal cream pie to the table. Rather than sit back down, she leaned a hip against her chair and kept a watch for the water to boil. "It's something about Thomas, isn't it? You know, I've prayed for him for so many years. In fact…" She tapped a finger against her chin. "I began praying for him in earnest after the fire."

Fern failed to see the link between the fire she'd started in her parents' kitchen and anything to do with Thomas Miller.

Her *mamm* turned her attention from the teapot and directly to Fern. "It was easy to remember to pray for him because I always prayed for him after I prayed for you."

Fern rubbed at her temples. She was confused, but also curious. "Why is that?"

"I believe Thomas blamed himself for Faith's death."

"But she died from complications of childbirth."

"Fern, guilt and blame are not always so cut and dry to the heart."

"But if he felt guilty, why would he leave his baby daughter?"

"I don't know, but I've seen that sometimes when someone feels guilty, they punish themselves. For some reason, Thomas thought his baby was better off without him—and maybe even that he was unworthy of her love. So, he refused it. Maybe he thought he'd get another chance someday. But then it was too late.

"Of course, I cannot claim to know what Thomas did or didn't feel. But I do know what happened to you. No one blamed you for what happened. No one punished you. But you punished yourself."

She had to admit that what her *mamm* said made some sense. Although it was much clearer to her in Thomas's case.

But her own?

Hasn't there been enough pain already? Had *Grossmammi* meant those words for Fern, too?

"It breaks a mother's heart to watch her child live her life believing that she is unworthy to be loved." Her *mamm*'s eyes misted. "I just keep praying."

The kettle whistled and her *mamm* paused to make the tea.

The choice is yours.

That couldn't be all. She couldn't just decide that Nick loved her. That was his choice, not hers.

But could she believe him if he did?

Guilt always seemed to sneak up on her whenever she thought she could finally be happy, telling her to make a hasty retreat before some awful thing happened.

Maybe she didn't need God to change Nick's heart. *Nay*, she needed Him to change her own. Apparently, love and happiness required a lot of faith. And her heart needed a God-sized portion.

Chapter Seventeen

An electric excitement buzzed among the growing gathering at Weaver's Store early Tuesday morning. Nick felt it humming in his own pulse. Even a television news crew from Roanoke had contacted the bishop about filming the story, promising to be discreet in their photo taking.

Nick worked his way around a huddle of Amish men from one of their neighboring mountain communities. Having spoken with them earlier to offer his gratitude for their help, he was aiming to do the same for several local construction workers. The men employed a few of the Amish men here today and graciously offered to lend their help, as well.

Someone tapped Nick on the shoulder.

He turned to see Eli.

"Just wanted to let you know there's been a minor change in plans. The women are still going to set up a water and refreshment table here. But I've sent the church wagon on up the road just a piece—where your old place borders this property. Thomas will oversee the setting up of tables and a few tents for shelter for the noon meal. There was a safety concern." Eli winked at him with that statement. "And it is getting almost too crowded for construction, much less so many tables and benches for a meal."

"Don't worry. I'll spread the word." Overtop of the crowd, Nick noticed the dawn's light getting brighter. "I believe we'll be able to begin soon."

Eli grinned widely. "*Ya, bruder*, the time has almost come."

Nick knew Eli didn't only mean for the hammering of nails and raising of wooden walls. He was fully aware of Nick's plan for their lunchtime break. And he'd taken extra effort to make sure there were as many witnesses as possible. The supposed safety concern was an excuse.

Nick could only hope that Fern was also pleased when the time came. In several scant hours, he'd find out. For now, there was a lot of work to be done.

* * *

Today, they were feeding as many people as they had on her wedding day. The meal wasn't as elaborate, but the labor was as tiring. Fern lifted her apron and dried her forehead.

And so much hotter.

"Can you carry these water pitchers to the tables, please?" Fern motioned to two of the school-age children helping with lunch. "Did the others return from the worksite yet?"

They shrugged they didn't know. She'd sent two of the oldest boys with the wagon to refill the cold drinks and salty treats for the construction crew. Hopefully, they hadn't gotten up to too much mischief. But more likely, they were of an age where they wanted to be in the middle of the excitement rather than helping with tasks that they deemed childish.

For the Amish, there was nothing so thrilling as a frolic like this one.

She blew at a stray hair that kept tickling her nose. Looking around to see if she'd missed the wagon's return, she noticed a plume of dust in the distance. As it neared, she could make out the crowd of men on the back of the flatbed.

Cupping her hands around her mouth, she called to the group of women under the tents ready to serve the meal. "Looks like they're arriving for lunch."

She scurried under the canopy erected to protect the food from the sun, welcoming the shade herself. Plastic wrap was lifted from sandwich platters, lids unscrewed off jars of Amish peanut butter spread, spoons plunged into bowls of macaroni and potato salad, and plates stacked high with plasticware rolled in napkins at the front of the lineup.

By the time they had everything ready, more men were arriving on foot through the field next to the back of the store. Careful not to stub her toes on the ice chests loaded with refills under the table, Fern took her place in the serving line.

She was exhausted, and the day was only half-done for all of them. That so many people would do this for them almost made her cry. Sure, she'd volunteered at frolics for others, and been happy to do so. But Nick was right that being on the receiving end was a vastly different and humbling experience. And she was so thankful he'd thought to suggest they give extra at the next collection of alms for the deacon's fund.

Her husband was an honorable man. And a generous one.

She glanced over the crowd, trying to find him. Having no success, she knew he'd come through the line eventually and looked forward to seeing him. Before long, the sounds of voices and laughter mingled to a fevered pitch. Folks from surrounding communities who hadn't seen their local family members in months huddled together. Hungry and giddy with the excitement of their morning achievements, everyone seemed to talk at once as they passed through the line.

The food disappeared as fast as the women assigned to refill it could manage replenishments. And Fern began to worry whether they'd prepared enough. But like the feeding of the five thousand, their tables were still filled with food after the last man was seated.

It was the first second she had to wonder again about Nick. Had she missed him in the chaos? The servers would eat soon, so she reached beneath the table for a fresh bowl of potato salad.

"What would you like to eat?" Nick's voice came down to her.

She bumped her head against the table, trying to stand. "I wondered what had happened to you." She came up holding a hand to the back of her head.

He was beside her with an empty plate, waiting to fill it for her. On church Sundays the men served the women, but today the ladies were going to fix their own, so the men could get back to work. Only Nick seemed to have a different idea.

"Have you even eaten? I didn't see you go through the line."

"As much as I could." He put on a reassuring smile, but the growl of his stomach contradicted him.

"Nick, you have to eat…"

"*Bitte*, Fern, let me serve you. You look like you could use a rest." When he asked like that, she couldn't refuse. But something seemed strange in the way he hurried to fix her plate and cleared a seat for her in the dead center of the front table.

She sat down with an uncomfortable feeling that more than one person was watching her. "Nick. What is this about?"

She asked too late. He'd already gone to stand in front of the serving table, and Eli was coming up beside him.

Eli's powerful strong voice settled the crowd as he called for everyone's attention, then introduced Nick *to say a few words*.

An uneasy dread crawled up her spine. This

wasn't how things went. There was an order they followed. And this… She didn't know what to make of it. But Nick had the undivided attention of every person present.

He thanked everyone for coming, and the knot in her middle eased. That was a thoughtful thing for him to do.

Fern picked up the slice of bread Nick had slathered with peanut butter spread. Her mouth was open for a bite when Nick began talking again.

"I realize my standing up here is an unusual thing. But today is an uncommon one for all of us. Raising a house, instead of a barn, has been somewhat tricky. And I want to thank the excellent work of all who took on the task of raising a house on top of a store, bringing it all to pass as we do things a little differently today.

"The way our people have rallied for my family out of compassion and concern may be the Amish way, but we are no less grateful for it. Without us ever asking, you rallied to do this kindness on our behalf, and when I gave the go-ahead, you showed up in numbers far more than I ever imagined." Nick had to clear his throat. And he wasn't the only one. In the pin-dropping silence, she heard several others in the crowd do so as well. Fern thought she may cry at the sincerity in his voice.

Then his gaze captured hers. A new kind of shiver ran up her spine. The warmth behind his eyes seemed to reach across the space between them. "Most of all, I thank *Gott* for giving me Fern to be my *frau*, who will turn this frame of a house you built today into a home. *Gott* has given me more than I could ever have asked for and all that I ever dreamed of."

A smattering of *amens* rippled through the crowd, which may as well have been a standing ovation by Amish standards. Fern held on to her chest with both hands in an effort to keep her heart inside.

There was no way to run from a declaration like that. And for once, she didn't want to.

"Take her up." Eli gave the order to lift the final wall. The workers knew his voice well enough, as he'd taken the role of foreman on many a project before, that he didn't need to shout. They were all ready for his command.

Arms outstretched and in unison with the others, Nick heaved. A few grunts sounded as the massive frame moved upward. Nothing compared to the feeling of such an accomplishment by team effort. A quiet awe took hold of them all as they momentarily soaked in the culmination of their efforts.

In the fleeting second, as Nick's eyes shut before the work continued, he saw but one face. Fern's. As he had spoken of her in front of the full gathering at lunch, he'd hoped above all hopes to settle once and for all in every Amish mind that he wanted Fern as his wife. He could never have chosen better. And whatever anyone thought about how their marriage began, he chose her now.

There'd been no time to tell her all he wished to privately, but he would as soon as he could steal her away after this was done.

Many hands make light work. Nick knew the saying well. But by the end of the day, he was sure all hands had put forth every ounce of effort they could muster. They were all exhausted as they left, but it was the best kind of tired.

"Spirits are highest when our bones are the weariest." Nick's *dat* clapped him on the back. "Hard work for the sake of another is the best kind. The memory of this day will carry us through many a harder one."

By us, Nick knew his *dat* meant the whole Amish community. "*Ya, Dat.* This has been a day I'll never forget."

Outsiders puzzled over their way of dress and their sacrifice of independence for community, but it was days like this that reminded them all of the security they had in bearing one another's burdens and the great things that their unity could accomplish.

"And Fern?" His *dat* gave him a point-blank stare. "I believe there is one more thing you need to say to your *frau* to make sure she never forgets this day, either."

A lump formed in Nick's throat. With all the good of his community, it also came with the downside that more often than not one's personal business became transparent to everyone.

"You're right. But I'd prefer a little privacy for that."

"Well, then, you'd best be on your way. I hear tell most all the helpers down by the food tents have left." His *dat* took hold of Nick's shoulders and gave him a prod in the direction of the field where Fern was likely finishing up her tasks. "And don't come home early."

Martin had helped Fern load the last of their supplies onto the wagon. Once the workers began leaving the store, her brother came to help her. Although he wasn't fooling her at all. Cassie was the last of the women here besides Fern.

"Can I help you up?" her brother asked as she was about to step up into the wagon next to Cassie.

"You know what? I believe a walk would do me wonders. And I'd like to go see the new house one more time." That was certainly true. It was awe-inspiring to see a whole new building attached to the back of the store where just this morning there'd been nothing but open air. She thought it may take some time to get used to seeing it—her home. *Ya,* she wanted to look at it one more time before dark.

"You two go on ahead." Fern wasn't surprised when neither offered an argument.

"Suit yourself." Martin shrugged, but Fern didn't miss the telltale smile of appreciation for her effort on his behalf.

Fern walked through the field toward the store. Toward home.

A frolic like this was always a heart-filling event. Today, though. *Ach!* Her heart may burst from the excitement of it all. She'd barely been able to concentrate on anything all afternoon other than Nick's speech.

What possessed a man to make a spectacle of himself like that? Every Amish family in districts for a hundred miles around were represented in that crowd. It was a very un-Amish thing to draw attention to oneself the way he had done. Yet, Eli had approved, even encouraged him.

And she couldn't be sorry for it, even if she had felt a tad self-conscious afterward. But not of anyone calling her *Poor Fern*.

Nay, no one was whispering *Poor Fern* now. Everyone knew her husband loved her. Because nothing else would have made him come forward to speak as he had.

Everyone knew. And she wouldn't be so foolish as to deny it any longer. It was a new and intoxicating feeling to embrace being loved like this. And as tired as she was from a long day of labor, her feet moved swiftly through the unmown hay brushing against her legs and swishing to the rhythm of her heart.

In the distance another form in the field took shape. Her steps quickened as she recognized Nick with his long, powerful strides headed her way.

"I'm sorry, Nick." The confession spilled as soon as they came face-to-face. "I'm so sorry for pushing you away."

"Hush." His warm palm, calloused from the day's work, wrapped around the scarred side of her neck, sending a shiver through her. "I don't need an apology, my love."

His love. Her heart truly might burst.

"*Bitte*, Nick. I need to apologize, if only this once. I suppose it was understandable after the accident when I withdrew. But then it must have become a habit—a bad one—of pushing you away. One I couldn't seem to stop. But I never stopped loving you. I buried that, too, but always it has been there. Always."

He swiped away a tear falling to her cheek. "And then the promises kept us from acknowledging what we both knew was true. I love you, Fern." He tilted his head down and rested his forehead against hers. And they remained there for several long and healing heartbeats.

Nick pulled back slightly. His blue eyes gazing deeply, as if down to her soul. "The promises weren't meant to separate us, Fern. They were always intended to bind us. She knew. Charity must have known. She designed each of our promises to bring us together.

"And with her blessing." He placed a gentle kiss on her cheek. "I was just too dense to understand until now."

"You were grieving. We both were." She reached her hand up to his face. "But I am so happy now. You make me more than happy,

Nick. You make me feel whole again. I love you."

His lips found hers. And she closed her eyes to the glow of the red sunset around them and leaned into the warmth of the man she loved and the delicious sweetness of being loved by him.

Epilogue

"Are you ready to see the inside?" Nick turned to Fern, who was studying the plot of land he'd fenced off for her garden.

Now that the field behind the store was back in the family, she could have as large of a vegetable garden as she wished and a greenhouse, too.

"Ya." She faced him, then took hold of Josh's hand.

"Not this time, *sohn*." Nick winked at his youngest. "This time your *mamm*'s hand will be held by me." And before any protests could arise, Nick swung Fern up into his arms. She sputtered and both of the *kinner* giggled. "You, my love, are going to be carried across the threshold."

She swatted at his shoulder with no genuine effort, then rested her hand on her tummy, making his heart skip a more joyful beat. Next year, they'd be a family of five.

Although the house had been framed in a single day, finishing the inside had taken a lot longer than the simpler task of completing a barn. Of course, Fern had overseen most of the process, but for the past week he'd made her stay away, so this moment could be more of a surprise.

"Look-see!" Josh swung the door open wide for Nick to carry Fern through.

Nick kissed her forehead and set her down inside the sunny downstairs room, then led them all upstairs.

Running her hands along the finished touches to the cabinets, Fern smiled. Then she saw the dining room table he'd had Rueben Bender craft for them. Her gaze drifted back to Nick. "Think of all the family meals and memories we will make. It is beautiful, Nick."

His heart swelled. He liked the thought of that, too. "One more thing. *Kumm.*"

Tugging on her hand, he pulled her to the room they would share and opened the door. His stomach knotted with nerves, hoping she liked what she saw.

With a small gasp, she placed her hand over her mouth, then went closer to the baby cradle on the floor at the foot of the bed. She bent down and rested her hand on the wooden side, rocking it. Her eyes were wide when she looked up at him. "*Ach*, Nick."

"Reuben helped me. He would've done a better job, but I wanted to make it myself."

"*Nay*, Nick, he couldn't have." She rose to stand in front of him. "Nothing could be more *wunderbar* than a gift made with such love."

Nick might have remained where he stood, basking in his *frau*'s tender kindness, if not for the squeals of his *kinner*.

"Does that mean we are going to have another brother or sister?" Bethany's eyes shone with glee.

"A *boppli*. A *boppli*." Josh bounced around the cradle. "I want a *bruder*."

Bethany's hands moved to her hips. "You don't get to decide. *Gott* does, and He will give me a sister."

"All right, you two." Fern laughed. "You'll see. It won't matter a bit when your baby brother or sister arrives, which one it is."

The *kinner* gave each other a skeptical look before Josh jumped around some more, singing, "A *boppli*. A *boppli*."

Nick shooed them both out of the room and stole a kiss from his beautiful, blushing *frau*.

* * * * *

Dear Reader,

Kumm mitt mich! Come with me for a visit to Promise, Virginia, a delightful Amish community nestled high above the Shenandoah Valley among the mountaintops of the Blue Ridge. The rural town of Promise is fictional, inspired by the Old Order Amish communities of the Virginia highlands and the centuries-old Mennonite heritage of the valley below.

Here, at Weaver's Amish Store, you'll meet Nick Weaver and Fern Beiler, along with their large families and many others in their cozy community—all connected through generations of coming together for the love and care of each other. I do hope you'll come back for more stories filled with faith and love from Promise.

I'd love to hear all about your visit with my friends on Promise Mountain. You can contact me through my website at amygrochowski. com.

With Love,
Amy

Get 3 FREE REWARDS!
We'll send you 2 FREE Books plus a FREE Mystery Gift.

FREE Value Over **$20**

Both the **Love Inspired®** and **Love Inspired® Suspense** series feature compelling novels filled with inspirational romance, faith, forgiveness and hope.

YES! Please send me 2 FREE novels from the Love Inspired or Love Inspired Suspense series and my FREE gift (gift is worth about $10 retail). After receiving them, if I don't wish to receive any more books, I can return the shipping statement marked "cancel." If I don't cancel, I will receive 6 brand-new Love Inspired Larger-Print books or Love Inspired Suspense Larger-Print books every month and be billed just $6.49 each in the U.S. or $6.74 each in Canada. That is a savings of at least 16% off the cover price. It's quite a bargain! Shipping and handling is just 50¢ per book in the U.S. and $1.25 per book in Canada.* I understand that accepting the 2 free books and gift places me under no obligation to buy anything. I can always return a shipment and cancel at any time by calling the number below. The free books and gift are mine to keep no matter what I decide.

Choose one:
☐ **Love Inspired Larger-Print**
(122/322 BPA GRPA)

☐ **Love Inspired Suspense Larger-Print**
(107/307 BPA GRPA)

☐ **Or Try Both!**
(122/322 & 107/307 BPA GRRP)

Name (please print)

Address   Apt. #

City   State/Province   Zip/Postal Code

Email: Please check this box ☐ if you would like to receive newsletters and promotional emails from Harlequin Enterprises ULC and its affiliates. You can unsubscribe anytime.

Mail to the Harlequin Reader Service:
IN U.S.A.: P.O. Box 1341, Buffalo, NY 14240-8531
IN CANADA: P.O. Box 603, Fort Erie, Ontario L2A 5X3

Want to try 2 free books from another series! Call 1-800-873-8635 or visit www.ReaderService.com.

Get 3 FREE REWARDS!

We'll send you 2 FREE Books <u>plus</u> a FREE Mystery Gift.

Both the **Harlequin® Special Edition** and **Harlequin® Heartwarming™** series feature compelling novels filled with stories of love and strength where the bonds of friendship, family and community unite.

YES! Please send me 2 FREE novels from the Harlequin Special Edition or Harlequin Heartwarming series and my FREE Gift (gift is worth about $10 retail). After receiving them, if I don't wish to receive any more books, I can return the shipping statement marked "cancel." If I don't cancel, I will receive 6 brand-new Harlequin Special Edition books every month and be billed just $5.49 each in the U.S. or $6.24 each in Canada, a savings of at least 12% off the cover price, or 4 brand-new Harlequin Heartwarming Larger-Print books every month and be billed just $6.24 each in the U.S. or $6.74 each in Canada, a savings of at least 19% off the cover price. It's quite a bargain! Shipping and handling is just 50¢ per book in the U.S. and $1.25 per book in Canada.* I understand that accepting the 2 free books and gift places me under no obligation to buy anything. I can always return a shipment and cancel at any time by calling the number below. The free books and gift are mine to keep no matter what I decide.

Choose one:
☐ **Harlequin Special Edition** (235/335 BPA GRMK)
☐ **Harlequin Heartwarming Larger-Print** (161/361 BPA GRMK)
☐ **Or Try Both!** (235/335 & 161/361 BPA GRPZ)

Name (please print)

Address _____ Apt. #

City _____ State/Province _____ Zip/Postal Code

Email: Please check this box ☐ if you would like to receive newsletters and promotional emails from Harlequin Enterprises ULC and its affiliates. You can unsubscribe anytime.

Mail to the Harlequin Reader Service:
IN U.S.A.: P.O. Box 1341, Buffalo, NY 14240-8531
IN CANADA: P.O. Box 603, Fort Erie, Ontario L2A 5X3

Want to try 2 free books from another series? Call 1-800-873-8635 or visit www.ReaderService.com.

*Terms and prices subject to change without notice. Prices do not include sales taxes, which will be charged (if applicable) based on your state or country of residence. Canadian residents will be charged applicable taxes. Offer not valid in Quebec. This offer is limited to one order per household. Books received may not be as shown. Not valid for current subscribers to the Harlequin Special Edition or Harlequin Heartwarming series. All orders subject to approval. Credit or debit balances in a customer's account(s) may be offset by any other outstanding balance owed by or to the customer. Please allow 4 to 6 weeks for delivery. Offer available while quantities last.

Your Privacy—Your information is being collected by Harlequin Enterprises ULC, operating as Harlequin Reader Service. For a complete summary of the information we collect, how we use this information and to whom it is disclosed, please visit our privacy notice located at corporate.harlequin.com/privacy-notice. From time to time we may also exchange your personal information with reputable third parties. If you wish to opt out of this sharing of your personal information, please visit readerservice.com/consumerschoice or call 1-800-873-8635. **Notice to California Residents**—Under California law, you have specific rights to control and access your data. For more information on these rights and how to exercise them, visit corporate.harlequin.com/california-privacy.

HSEHW23